3 8002 01492 8032

KT-578-249

COVENTRY LIBRARIES
WITHDRAWN
FOR SALE

The Vernon Brand

The Vernon Brand is going to be the biggest in the territory and Harry Vernon's plans are working out well. Then rustling starts and a stage-coach is held up with some of Harry's money on board. Phil Jones is the Elverton deputy marshal and Harry's nephew. He soon has one of the hold-up men in the jail house, but somebody frees the man.

Then the marshal is brutally murdered and the young deputy finds himself on the trail of the killers. Soon to follow is a vicious range war and not until the mystery is solved can lasting peace return to a troubled land.

The Vernon Brand

Tom Benson

A Black Horse Western

ROBERT HALE · LONDON

© Tom Benson 2007
First published in Great Britain 2007

ISBN 978-0-7090-8317-7

Robert Hale Limited
Clerkenwell House
Clerkenwell Green
London EC1R 0HT

The right of Tom Benson to be identified as
author of this work has been asserted by him
in accordance with the Copyright, Designs and
Patents Act 1988

COVENTRY CITY LIBRARIES	
201492803	
HJ	21/03/2007
F	£11.25
CEN	AA 20/6/07

Typeset by
Derek Doyle & Associates, Shaw Heath
Printed and bound in Great Britain by
Antony Rowe Limited, Wiltshire

ONE

The marshal was a big man. He dwarfed the cow pony that bore his weight with stoic calm. Eli Anderson was new at the job. He had been chosen by the people of Elverton after the last marshal left town amid stories of extorting money from the local store owners. Folk decided that they needed an honest man for a change. They still had to put up with the mayor and his cronies until the next election, but they could at least change the marshal.

He watched now as the long string of cattle passed slowly to new pasture in the valley below. The calls of the ranch hands drifted up on the breeze and the owner of the vast spread was sitting his own horse next to the marshal.

Harry Vernon was a slight figure, stooped in the saddle and with a weather-tanned face that showed every trace of his sixty years of a hard life. His watering eyes were a pale blue and a hooked nose dominated the lined face. He was neatly dressed and freshly shaven, but a certain slyness took something away from the features of somebody who should have been a pillar of the local community. He waved a hand towards the moving cattle.

'You see what I'm up against, Eli,' he grumbled. 'There's fifteen fellas out there all the time, but we ain't got eyes in our asses. I've lost near five hundred head in the last few months, and Vic Lawrence reckons to have lost almost as many. Art Rubin's missin' three hundred or so and he's as mad as a bull fenced off from the cows. You law fellas just ain't much help.'

Marshal Anderson grinned reluctantly. 'I got me just one deputy, as you very well know, Harry,' he said quietly. 'And we have a town to run and no legal rights outside it. This is work for Sheriff Haynes and the county. But I figure as how you already know that. What I'm really wonderin' is why you asked me to ride out here. It sure ain't to admire the view.'

Harry Vernon's pale eyes held the hint of a smile.

'Well, you could be right, Eli,' he said. 'It's about that nephew of mine. I need the young fool here, not struttin' round Elverton totin' a gun and punchin' drunks in the head. What sorta life is that for a fella with his background? My sister's boy is the best shot and the best horseman in the family. With all this rustlin' goin' on, I sure as hell need him back on the spread. You can always get yourself another deputy. There's enough fellas in town eager to earn a few dollars for wearin' a badge. This cattle thievin' is a serious business.'

'You got two sons workin' for you, Harry. What about them?'

The rancher snorted with contempt. 'Hal and Vinnie take after their ma's side of the family. If a flea bit them they wouldn't know where the hell to scratch. Why Phil decided not to work for me, I just can't figure. He could be part of the biggest spread in the territory. I've got plans for the future that you wouldn't believe.'

'Maybe that's why he's workin' for me,' the marshal suggested drily.

'You'd be meanin' that I ain't the honestest fella in the world?'

'Harry, you're as twisted as an angry rattler. Phil's ma brought him up all churchgoin' and knowin' right from wrong. That's why I accepted Phil as my deputy when he asked for the job. You gotta let the lad run his own life. He don't want to be a rancher.'

Harry nodded reluctantly. 'You could be right,' he admitted, 'but at least have a word with him. He ain't gonna be more than a deputy marshal for a coon's age. You got years to go yet and he could do one hell of a lot better workin' for me. He's gonna own part of the spread when I go, anyways. He'll get his ma's share. That's how my old man arranged it. Lookit, Eli. I got plans to buy up Les Weldon's place, and I'm gettin' in some new stud bulls this comin' season. My brand will be the only one you'll see for a hundred miles in any direction.'

'You sure got big ideas, Harry,' the marshal said drily. 'It's all gonna cost a lotta money.'

The rancher nodded. 'It sure is, and that's why I need to do somethin' about this rustlin' we been gettin' lately. I gotta go crawlin' to that money-lendin' bastard at the bank to raise a few thousand dollars. I've also had to do a deal on my sister's hotel in Phoenix to get my hands on some more cash money. That's comin' into town on the next stage.'

The marshal blinked rapidly. He sensed a sudden danger in the conversation.

'Harry,' he said slowly, 'I thought Mary's place would belong to Phil after she died.'

'Well, it does,' the rancher agreed reluctantly, 'but he ain't made a move to sell it, and he don't take no interest in it, so I raised a loan on the deeds. They was left with me and he's content to just collect a monthly slice of the profits that the manager banks for him. He shoulda sold the place. It would make an almighty good saloon or whorehouse.'

'And does Phil know about this?'

Harry gave a slight grin.

'Well, I ain't seen him so as to mention it,' he admitted, 'but I don't reckon a nice honest lad like Phil would begrudge his old uncle a loan to increase the family wealth.'

'And if he was under your eye at the ranch, it'd be easier to get him round to your way of thinking,' the marshal muttered sourly.

'I ain't reckonin' on cheatin' him, Eli,' the rancher protested. 'He gets a share of the spread when I die and I figure as how he should pull his weight in buildin' it up. Let's face it, we're all kin, and I lent Mary the money to buy that place in Phoenix.'

Eli Anderson pulled a face. 'And that's another thing, Harry,' he said sharply. 'This money that's comin' into Elverton on the stage. I hope it's one of them bank draft things and not solid cash.'

'It's solid cash, man. The fella I'm buyin' the new bulls from wants ready money. It's a good deal and I don't aim to argue with him. You got some objections to that?'

'Well, stages have been known to meet up with some pretty rough fellas when they're carryin' large amounts of money. Who the hell knows about this fool trick?'

'Nobody. Do you think I'm some pantywaist who don't understand these things? The stage gets into Elverton on Thursday as usual. I checked to make sure it was just a normal run. A few dollars and some papers for the bank. Then there's the mail delivery but no big money. So me and the Wells Fargo fellas made arrangements to keep it secret between ourselves. We don't go talkin' in saloons or whisperin' things on the pillows in a whorehouse. Nobody but you and me knows that money is comin' into town. That stage ain't worth spittin' on, never mind holdin' up.'

'Well, I hope you're right, Harry. I'd rather die of boredom than gun fights.'

TWO

The stage moved fast over the dry ground. It threw up a cloud of dust that billowed behind it like some great brown haze to hang on the air. There were four passengers on board and the six mules pulled heartily as they stretched their legs for the first time in days. They had been freshly hitched up at the last halt and responded to the reins with eagerness.

The trail rose gradually towards the rougher ground ahead. There was scrub and several stands of dried sycamores that housed birds of prey watching every movement in the barren land-scape. The driver urged his animals on as the stage lumbered up to a ridge and then began to travel more easily down the gentle slope towards a denser mass of tall cactus plants.

It was there that the five men were waiting. They rode out from behind cover and fired their pistols into the air. The guard on the stage raised his scatter-gun but had no chance. One of the riders caught him with a single shot and he rolled off his seat to the ground below.

The driver took no risks. He tugged at the reins and raised one hand towards the heavens in token of surrender. The large stage gradually drew to a rumbling halt and the passengers peered fearfully out from behind the leather blinds.

'Throw down the strongbox,' the leader of the gang shouted as he waved a gun at the driver.

The man complied and the metal container hit the earth amid a few whoops from the hold-up men. One of them dismounted and took a hammer and chisel from his saddle-bag. It only needed a few blows to detach the heavy padlock and allow the kneeling man to display the loot. There were some bags of newly minted coins and two bundles of notes that amounted to $300 or $400. The rest of the contents were legal papers of various sorts.

The leader of the gang swore vividly and got down from his horse. He threw open the door of the stage and ordered the passengers to get out.

There were three scared men and one woman. They stood in a row, their hands raised and panic on their faces.

'You get down too, fella,' the leader ordered the driver.

He watched while the man scrambled from the box and then grabbed him by the collar.

'There was money put on this stage,' he hissed with his face close to the scared driver. 'Now it ain't in the strongbox, so it gotta be some place else. So let's do it the easy way and you just tell me where it is.'

The driver shook his head violently. His voice trembled as he spoke.

'That's all they put on board. I swear it is,' he whined. 'All these folks saw the Wells Fargo man and the bank agent give me the box. There ain't no more, fella. I swear it.'

The gang leader stood for a moment as though undecided. He was a short, heavily built man of middle age with a dark face and pale-grey eyes that flickered angrily over the scene. He looked at the passengers as he let go of the driver.

'Search the stage,' he ordered his men, 'and go through the baggage these folks is carrying. Them dollars has to be somewhere on this rig.'

He weighed each of the travellers up carefully as the gang carried out his orders. The three men were middle-aged and dusty as well as frightened. Two were dressed as town folk and one of them, a little fellow with glasses and tufts of grey hair sticking out from under his hat, was shivering. The woman was elderly, heavily built and neatly dressed. The gang leader eyed the brooch attached to her high collar and decided not to bother with it. He just held them all in a line by the mules while the stage was thoroughly searched.

One of the gang even emptied the feed bags and pulled out the leather seat cushions. They found nothing. The baggage was emptied out on to the trail as they went through the leather valises and carpetbags. One item held the attention of a grinning gunman as he opened it up to display two rows of small bottles.

He took one out and looked at the label. The fact that he could not read did not really worry him. He removed the cork and sniffed the contents.

'Whiskey,' he crooned as he took a swallow of the precious fluid.

'They're my samples!' the little man shrieked. He made to rush forward but the gun waved him back. 'Please don't drink them. I'll have nothing to show the folk in town.'

'You a whiskey-drummer?' one of the other men asked as he joined his mate at the leather bag.

'Yes, and they're my living. Please don't drink them. I've got money in my wallet. All of twenty dollars. Take that, fella, but don't damage the samples.'

There was a chorus of derisive laughter as more bottles were opened. All the robbers agreed that it

14

was good stuff; better than the watered-down rubbish in the average saloon. They had a few more swigs until their boss brought them angrily to order. The passengers were made to empty out their watches, money, and anything else of value while the bag of whiskey samples was dropped to the ground with a heart-rending sound of breaking glass. The little man almost sobbed as he stood with his hands raised.

The boss of the gang took a final look round. His dark face showed the anger he felt at not finding what he was looking for. He waved the passengers back into the stage and told the driver to get the hell out of it. The dead guard's watch and guns were collected, along with his tobacco pouch. His brass vesta case was spurned.

Some of the baggage still lay on the ground but the little whiskey-drummer had picked up his damaged samples and wrapped towels round what was left of them. He almost wept as he nursed the leather bag and climbed back into his seat. The woman passenger cast a sorrowful glance at her scattered belongings but consoled herself with the thought that most of her money was safely hidden in her stays. And she was wearing them.

The gang mounted their horses as the mules sprang into action once more and carried off the pillaged vehicle in a cloud of dust.

'We was sure sold short,' one of the gang grumbled as he picked over the watch chains and vesta boxes in his damp hands. 'That fella you got the lead from needs a bullet in the butt, and mighty quick, Harry.'

The boss shook his head as he swung his horse round to gallop away.

'He told us what he knew,' he snapped angrily. 'It's them bankin' fellas in Phoenix. They just didn't put the money on board. Maybe they got some other way of deliverin' or maybe they aim to use the next stage.'

'Well, I don't figure to be holdin' up another stage round here,' one of the gang yelled as they moved off. 'This trail will be as hot as a preacher's dream of hell.'

The leader reined in his horse and looked hard at the man.

'Yeah, you got somethin' there,' he conceded. 'We'll camp near Elverton and I'll clean up a bit and ride into town. All the folks on that stage will have passed through by then and nobody ain't gonna bother about a clean-lookin' ranch hand just havin' a quiet drink.'

The others laughed as their boss rubbed his unshaven face.

'If we make camp by the creek, you can have an all-over wash,' one of them suggested. 'You'll sure smell prettier.'

The atmosphere seemed lightened a little as they rode off.

The stage was already in Elverton. It had come clattering in at a greater speed than usual, and that alone was enough to attract attention. But it was the missing guard and the shouts of the driver that really brought people running towards the dust-covered vehicle as it drew up outside the marshal's office instead of the Wells Fargo depot.

Marshal Anderson was dozing in his chair until the noise woke him up. He glanced through the grimy windows and saw the mules drawing to a halt amid a flurry of shouts and sprays of foam from their sweating mouths. He hitched up his pants and headed for the door, just pausing for a moment to put on his hat and wipe his eyes with a soiled bandanna.

'What in hell's happened, Doug?' he shouted to the driver as the man fastened the reins round the brake lever.

'We been held up, Marshal, and Ted Larby's dead,' the driver shouted back as he descended and began his tale. The passengers joined in and the whole town seemed to be standing around listening to the news.

Eli Anderson eventually got the driver and passengers into the privacy of his office while a couple of councilmen kept the excited townsfolk

17

beyond the closed door. The mayor had hurried over to sit in on events and the story was gradually told in a more level-headed and lucid manner. It was the woman who gave the best description of the hold-up men. She was Ma Quilly, the widow of a judge and, as she told those around her, highly respected by all the powerful men in politics. The little whiskey-drummer was worse than useless. He dithered as he squirmed on the bentwood chair. His damaged samples sat on his lap, the stains of whiskey seeping through the bag to wet his knees. The smell added to the musty atmosphere of the marshal's office.

Eli Anderson made notes while the mayor postured in his usual manner. Banker Halliday arrived to see what had happened to the few hundred dollars he was expecting. He was also concerned about the mail and various documents. His stout figure exuded sweat as he became more outraged at how little protection the stage possessed.

It was an hour before the office cleared again and Eli was left to contemplate what must have happened to Harry Vernon's money. Nobody had mentioned it and the rancher would almost certainly be coming into town to collect it. An angry Harry Vernon was not a welcome thought.

The elderly Wells Fargo agent had spent his time more usefully. He organized the recruitment of a new guard, made sure the mules were fed and watered, and then checked to see which of the passengers would continue the journey. Ma Quilly announced herself too shaken to travel and was directed to the Morrison House Hotel. The male passengers all elected to continue the journey, and eventually clambered back on board.

Nobody took much notice of the little whiskey-drummer. He sidled into the Wells Fargo office after the others had left and put his ravaged sample-bag on the counter.

'I'd like to leave this here,' he said meekly. 'The other passengers might find the smell unpleasant, and there's too much damage for me to take it any further.'

The clerk nodded sympathetically. 'I'll get rid of it for you, sir,' he said.

He put the bag under the counter and reached for a cloth to wipe the marks it left on the wood-work. The drummer nodded his thanks and left to board the stage. Harry Vernon's money had arrived safely.

Marshal Anderson stood at the window of his office and thought over the happenings of the day. He watched the stage depart and glanced at the Eli Woods clock on the wall to note the time. It would be dark in a couple of hours, and they would have to travel the last few miles to the next stop in difficult conditions. He shrugged his shoulders and went back to the desk. He had other problems on his mind.

Ma Quilly had problems as well. She booked into the Morrison House and had a quick meal from a sympathetic management. Then she went shopping to replace what she had lost when her baggage was left strewn over the trail. She was a tough woman and the spending of money calmed what trace of nerves she had experienced. She eventually went back to the hotel for supper and settled down in her room to read the newly arrived newspaper.

Reaction to the events of the day began to set in and her eyes grew tired in the lamplight. She crossed to the window to pull the drapes and cut out some of the noise on the main street. There were plenty of people about and the Golden Bell saloon was almost opposite across the rutted thoroughfare. It was a warm evening and the saloon was busy, with the sound of a piano and some shouting from a couple of early drunks.

She shook her head in righteous displeasure and was about to turn away when something caught her attention. She had seen somebody she recognized.

THREE

Eli Anderson was cooking himself a bit of supper on the pot-bellied stove. Writing up his report on the stage hold-up had given him a long night and he knew that his wife would be asleep when he arrived home. He was frying bacon and making coffee. There was some slightly stale bread but he was hungry enough to tackle anything.

The office was warm and the windows were steamed up. The opening of the door drew in a blast of cold night air and the marshal almost cursed to be caught with a skillet in his large hands. The intruder was the woman from the stage. He struggled for a moment to recall her name as he put down the pan and tried to smile at the interruption.

'Well, this is unexpected, Mrs Quilly,' he said as he hastily stood in front of his cooking efforts. 'What can I be doin' for you at this time of night?'

21

'I just seen one of them hold-up fellas, Marshal,' the woman said breathlessly. 'Seen him as plain as daylight, right across the street from my window.'

The marshal looked hard at the woman. His first thought was that she was hysterical, but as he scanned her determined face and recalled her comparative coolness when she arrived in town, he decided to take her seriously.

'Where was he?' he asked in a low voice.

'I just saw him from my window. He was goin' into that dreadful saloon across the street.'

Marshal Anderson crossed ponderously to the desk and picked up his gunbelt.

'You sure it was him, ma'am?' he asked as he strapped it on. 'I don't want to go makin' trouble for some harmless ranch hand.'

'Sure I'm sure,' the woman spat angrily. 'I ain't blind and my ma didn't raise no idiot children. He'd had a shave and a good wash, but the shirt's the same and that battered nose of his ain't out of a picture gallery. He just got off the same cow pony he was ridin' at the stage and went up them steps. You go get him, Marshal.'

'You'll have to come along with me, lady,' Eli Anderson said as he ushered her to the door, 'and point him out to me.'

Ma Quilly bridled angrily. 'I ain't goin' in any saloon,' she snapped. 'I'm a God-fearin' woman. . . !'

'Just point him out through the window,' the marshal told her patiently. 'Then I'll go in and question him.'

The two walked down the street and across to the Golden Bell. A few people looked curiously at the couple and folks began to get interested when Ma Quilly mounted the boardwalk and peered through the steamy windows of the brightly lit saloon. They saw her jab a finger against the glass and they drew nearer to try and catch the conversation between her and the marshal.

Then they watched her follow the lawman as he headed towards the swing-doors. She stopped at the threshold while Eli Anderson pushed past a slightly drunk cowhand and entered the warmth of the Golden Bell.

He could see the man he wanted. A short, thickset fellow who leaned on the bar with a whiskey-glass in his hand. He appeared relaxed and harmless enough, but there was a gun at his belt and his pale eyes were alert and checking the saloon as if looking for someone. The marshal was losing his doubts as he watched. The man was certainly a stranger and his air of ease was an assumed one. There seemed to be some sort of tension about him. Eli Anderson checked his gun and crossed the saloon.

The man stiffened at the sight of the marshal, and if Eli had any doubts about Ma Quilly's identification, they were stilled by the sudden tension.

'You're a stranger in town, fella,' the lawman said quietly. 'What brings you to Elverton?'

The man put down his glass so that his right hand was free.

'Just passin' through,' he said. 'I'm camped outside town and I thought as how I'd come in for a drink. Don't aim to make no trouble, Marshal, and I can pay my way.'

'Glad to hear it. It's just that we had the stage held up today and strangers is a bit of interest to me right now. What do you work at?'

'Ranch hand. I'm on my way to the KT spread out at Polver's Creek.'

'Is that a fact? Well, now, I'd like you to help me out a little. There are some folks still in town who were on the stage today. I want one of them to see you. If she can tell me that you had nothin' to do with the hold-up, you can finish your drink in peace. And I'll be happy to buy you one myself.'

The man moved slightly away from the bar counter.

'I don't like folk suggestin' that I'm some sorta thief,' he said in a low, controlled voice. 'All I came in here for was a quiet drink. I ain't pickin' fights with nobody, but I ain't runnin' from trouble either. I suggest you go get those folks and bring them here. I aim to finish this whiskey.'

'Well, I'd rather that you came along to the jailhouse. My informant is a woman, and she ain't enterin' a saloon. You know how the ladies are about drinkin' places like this. It won't take more than a few minutes.'

The man straightened up and seemed about to comply. Then something caught his eye and a look of alarm passed across the dark face. He had caught a glimpse of Ma Quilly peering in at the door. Before the marshal could react, the man's gun flew to his hand and as the other drinkers stumbled over each other to get out of range, a single shot was fired and a thin spiral of smoke drifted up towards the ceiling.

Marshal Anderson had drawn his own gun almost as quickly. But he was too late, and as his thumb pulled back the hammer, he felt a heavy blow at the top of his left arm. He staggered against the bar counter. His left hand moved as though without control. It struck a couple of glasses and scattered the contents as the glasses rolled off to the floor and smashed.

The stranger turned from the marshal and waved his gun wildly around at the other drinkers. They scattered as he ran to the door and pushed through to the stoop. He swung back and fired one warning shot to discourage any pursuit. Then he unhitched his cow pony and swung into the saddle.

It was then that things went wrong. The saddle

slid round as his foot put pressure on the stirrup. His left hand was clutching the pommel and his right still held the gun. He lost his grip, the Colt flew across the far side of the horse as the man slid almost to his knees and got tangled with the reins. He started to struggle to his feet and found a man standing over him.

Deputy Marshal Phil Jones was a tall young fellow with fair hair and widely set grey eyes that now looked down at the man on the ground. The lawman held a pistol steadily and the sound of the hammer being pulled back was loud in the silence that seemed to fall on the watchers.

'Folks what leave their horses outside a saloon for a long time usually loosen the girth,' the deputy marshal said in a quiet, conversational voice. 'You musta forgot to do it, so I thought as how I'd help out. Suppose we take a walk to the jailhouse and you tell me why you just shot the marshal.'

The man got to his feet. He looked longingly at the gun that now lay between the hoofs of his horse, then slowly walked towards the marshal's office. The mayor was now on the scene and Doctor Harper was hurrying up the steps to tend to the injured lawman. People were gathering again, crowding around now that there was no fear of any more shooting. They threatened the stranger and some blows were struck as Phil Jones pushed through to get the man to the safety of a cell.

Ma Quilly followed the deputy marshal waving a triumphant arm.

'That's him!' she shouted enthusiastically. 'I'd know him anywhere. He's for a hanging.'

Phil Jones soon had his prisoner behind bars. After completing that task he took the overheated skillet off the stove and opened the rear door of the building to take away the smell of the smoking and overcooked bacon. The mayor arrived a few minutes later. He was accompanied by the judge who had been in the saloon and walked with some difficulty as he steered himself to the only available bentwood chair.

'Eli's got a broken arm,' Mayor Raynor informed young Phil as he searched the marshal's desk for whiskey. 'He won't be marshallin' for some time. If at all. We're gonna need a new marshal.'

'We got one right here,' Judge Murphy mumbled as he watched the First Citizen pour out the drinks.

'Phil here is too young for them responsibilities,' Mayor Raynor said dismissively. 'I was thinkin' of Ed Welsey.'

'Your nephew?' The judge laughed at the idea. 'The last marshal was kin to you, and look what happened. The folks would never allow it, Bert.'

'I had no part to play in that affair,' the mayor stuttered angrily. 'I just do what I think is best for the town.'

'I reckon the marshal will be back at work as soon as his arm's healed,' Phil Jones said without rancour. 'After all, he don't shoot with his left hand.'

'Ain't that the truth.' The judge chuckled as he held out his glass for a refill. 'Now, suppose you tell us what all this is about, young fella. I ain't been so well entertained since the preacher fell down the privy.'

Phil glanced across at the prisoner who sat disconsolately on his bunk.

'This fella and four others raided the stage. Then they rode off and made camp just outside town. Close by Bennet's Creek. I was gonna come back here, get a posse together, and go round 'em up. Then this fella gets all shaved and washed, and sets out for town. I was sure puzzled so I just followed, all careful-like.'

The mayor looked at the judge and held up a restraining hand.

'Hold it there, young fella,' he said. 'How come you was on the spot? Just passin' by?'

'No, Mr Mayor. Marshal Anderson sent me to trail the stage after it left the last halt. Y'see, somebody told him that there was gonna be a lotta cash money on board. I think it was Harry Vernon. We

28

got no powers outside town, but the marshal reckoned as how I could at least keep what he called a watchin' brief on things. So there I was followin' the stage when these five fellas hold it up. There weren't nothin' I could do against five of them, so I just kept watch.'

The mayor nodded his understanding and the judge lifted his glass in a hazy salute.

'When this fella comes into town, he goes straight to the Golden Bell saloon,' the deputy continued. 'I reckoned as how it weren't no casual sorta thing. He musta had a reason, so I watched from outside to see who he was meetin' there.'

The mayor let out a grunt of approval.

'And did he meet someone?' he asked eagerly.

'No. Marshal Anderson and that woman who was on the stage came stormin' across the street. She points through the window and then he goes into the saloon. I'd already loosened the girth on the fella's horse, and before I could do anythin' else, they was shootin' it out.'

The judge coughed and there was a crafty look in his watery eyes.

'I was there when all this happened,' he said, 'and the marshal weren't shot right away. You must have seen him talkin' to this fella. Am I right?'

Phil Jones nodded.

'And you wondered if the marshal was the man this bandit had come to meet?'

Phil smiled. 'That did cross my mind,' he admitted.

'You got an old head on them young shoulders,' the judge conceded. 'With a little education, you'd have made a good lawyer.'

'There ain't no good lawyers,' the mayor snorted. He turned to Phil. 'And did this fella talk to anybody in the saloon?'

'No, he didn't have time. He'd just settled down with a drink when the marshal arrived with the woman.'

'They kinda spoiled things, didn't they?' the judge wheezed. 'So we're none the wiser.'

The mayor got to his feet. The bottle was empty and it was past his bedtime.

'I reckon that Eli will beat it outa him when he gets back from Doc Harper's butcher-shop. If he can't manage it with one hand, young fella, you'll have to give him some help. If somebody in Elverton is passin' information to hold-up men, we need to know.'

The judge stood up as well, obliging the mayor to help him keep upright.

'I can't be hearin' things like this,' he said. 'I gotta give this bastard a fair trial before we hang him. You did a fine job, young Phil. I'll wish you a good night.'

'Before you go,' the deputy said urgently, 'there's one more thing to settle. The other four

30

fellas are still out at Bennet's Creek. We gotta get a posse together and go catch 'em. I need your authority, Mr Mayor.'

The First Citizen looked undecided as he stood in the doorway.

'At this time of night?' he mused. 'I don't figure on folk bein' too keen to volunteer. And posse money don't come cheap. The street's lookin' deserted now and it'd be one hell of a ride out to the creek without some decent moonlight. They'll hear you comin' and be away or up and fightin' before you're on to them. Let's leave it be. We got the fella who's probably the boss man. What do you say, Pat?'

The judge gave it his judicial consideration before nodding his head.

'One hangin's expensive enough,' he said firmly. 'Let's go get some sleep. It's been a good night's work and we can rest in peace.'

The door closed behind the two men and Phil went to shut the rear door of the building. Most of the smell had gone and he put on some coffee. The prisoner sat miserably and paid no attention even when the door opened again and Marshal Anderson entered. His left arm was in a sling and covered in a plaster cast. He looked a little pale after the attentions of the doctor, but gave Phil a cheerful grin.

'I could sure as hell use that coffee, young fella,'

he said as he lowered himself awkwardly into his chair. 'And with a spot of somethin' stronger in it.'

He looked at the empty whiskey-bottle and shook his head in mock despair.

'Looks like you've had a visit from the mayor,' he mused as he searched the desk for another bottle.

'And the judge,' Phil told him.

'Lucky they left this.' The marshal pulled out another bottle and opened it thankfully. 'The doc said I weren't to take no liquor for a day or two. But then the doc ain't got a broken arm. Just pass me that coffee.'

Only when the marshal had taken a deep draught of the brew did he turn his attention to the man in the cell.

'Well, I reckon as how you've already been promised a hangin' for the shootin' of Ted Larby,' he said quietly, 'but folks on the spot tell me that you was lookin' for some money you think shoulda been on that stage. Now that was a little secret between the fella who sent it and the fella who was to collect it. So somebody has to be tellin' tales.'

The prisoner did not answer.

'Now, I ain't feelin' well enough to ask questions right now,' the marshal went on, 'so you can keep your teeth until morning. But I'm tellin' you, fella, somebody back in Phoenix has been talkin' outa school. It ain't our local Wells Fargo clerk.

He's too old and honest for that. But I reckon you got somebody up north on your payroll. So get some sleep, and we'll do the same.'

He turned to Phil. 'I reckon you and me is stayin' here the night,' he said. 'I don't want the rest of this fella's gang turnin' up like Custer and his bluebellies. We're gonna draw the shutters and lock them doors. We'll take turns to sleep and keep one of the lamps burnin' all night. Load the shotguns and lay 'em out ready. I'd hate this bird to fly the nest. Not after what he did to me.'

He went to the desk and put the whiskey-bottle back in the drawer. Then he looked hard at Phil.

'You musta seen me go into the saloon,' he said thoughtfully.

'I did.'

'Yeah, and you wondered if I might be the fella this bozo was tryin' to contact?'

'I was suspicious of everybody. He had to have a real good reason for comin' into town. Nothin' personal, Marshal.'

'And no offence taken, lad. You were quite right, and you got the makings of a good lawman. Go get some sleep. I'll keep watch for a coupla hours. That other cell's got clean blankets and I'll turn the wick down a bit. I'll wake you when I start noddin' off myself. This arm's achin' one hell of a lot so I ain't feelin' like beddin' down just yet.'

Phil helped the marshal draw the shutters and

33

make sure that the doors were locked. Then he retired to the cell adjoining the one occupied by the prisoner. The straw mattress was comfortable and he was quickly off to sleep.

The shot seemed deafening and Phil Jones jarred awake with a gasp as he tried to make sense of things. He could hear shouts and curses as he went to join the marshal who was trying to unlock the door of the other cell. The prisoner was on his knees with blood pouring from the left side of his face and shoulder. He moaned something and pointed to the high, barred window.

Phil rushed to the front door and began unlocking it. He let in a blast of cold air as he stumbled out to the boardwalk with a Colt .44 in his hand and cocked ready for use. The main street was deserted as he ran round the side of the building. The little alley was alive with rats that scuttled from his sight.

There was no sign of another human being. Whoever had fired through the window of the cell had got away in the darkness. There was an upturned wooden pail below the barred window, and that seemed to be what the marksman had stood on when he fired through at the prisoner.

Phil ran back and joined the marshal who was now tending the man's wounds. He had been peppered with buckshot. The right side of his face and shoulder were badly torn. He writhed as the lawman helped him on to the bunk and applied a large bandanna to the worst area of bleeding.

The doctor soon showed up. He took over while Phil turned up the wick of the main oil-lamp and lit one of the others to help brighten up the scene. The mayor arrived a little time later. He had wisely waited in case there was any more shooting. He and the marshal stood by the desk while Phil helped the doctor.

'I reckon some folk just ain't prepared to wait for a hanging,' the mayor said as he looked hope-fully towards the drawer where the whiskey-bottles were kept. 'Ted Larby was a popular man.'

The marshal took out the bottle and poured a drink for them both.

'I don't figure it that way,' he said quietly. 'I can't go into details, but this fella had an infor-mant. I reckoned as how his contact was back in Phoenix, but this shootin' tells me that he ain't. The fella's right here in town, and scared to hell that his name's gonna be mentioned.'

FOUR

Harry Vernon rode into town the next day. He was escorted by five of his hands and all were carrying Winchester carbines. They passed the jailhouse without interest and stopped at the office of Wells Fargo. Harry dismounted and went inside.

Old Vic Dyson was behind the counter writing out parcel labels. He looked up with a toothless grin when Harry arrived. The two men just nodded to each other, then the clerk reached under the counter and produced the battered sample-bag. It still smelt a little but Harry took it thankfully and tipped the man a dollar. He was about to turn and leave when Vic raised a hand to stop him.

'You almost lost that,' he croaked. 'The stage was held up.'

Harry's face hardened. 'Is that a fact now? So what exactly happened?'

Vic told him and the rancher listened without interruption. When he left the office he walked along the boardwalk to the jailhouse. His escort accompanied him, one of them leading their boss's horse.

Marshal Anderson was at his desk when the door flew open and Harry Vernon stormed in. He looked at the wounded lawman and then at Phil Jones, who was making coffee.

'I've just heard tell of this hold-up,' he said angrily. 'That stage was carryin' nothin' worth a Confederate dollar, so somebody musta talked about my money.'

He crossed to the cell and glared at the prisoner.

'Has this fella talked yet?'

The marshal shook his head. 'No. He won't even give us his own name. He's just bein' plain dumb. But don't worry, Harry. As soon as I feel a little better, I'll be askin' him again. All nice and friendly-like. He'll talk.'

The marshal got up and crossed to stand next to his visitor.

'Are you sure you ain't been talkin' yourself?' he asked.

'I ain't spoke to nobody. Not even my hands knew what the hell was goin' on. It has to be some fella in the Phoenix office of Wells Fargo. And I wants to know who.'

37

'Don't we all? But I don't reckon to it bein' Phoenix.'

The marshal explained about the shooting and Harry Vernon listened with furrowed brows. He banged the sample-bag down on the desk and the remaining bottles rattled noisily. The prisoner looked up sharply as he suddenly realized where the money had been hidden.

'Well, it can't be old Vic Dyson,' Harry said as he turned away from the bandaged man in the cell. 'So who the hell could know? I'm tellin' you, Eli, I never uttered a word about the shipment. Anyway, it arrived safely and I got me a good escort outside. The fella is comin' over to the ranch with the stud bulls, and once the deal is done, I'll rest easy. Then we can see if his animals are as good as he says they are.'

'I still can't figure why the two of you ain't usin' the bank,' the marshal mused.

Harry grinned. 'Ain't my doing, fella. I figure as how the seller don't want that bankin' bastard to know he's got ready cash. Probably owes him money, but I don't ask questions. It don't pay.'

He nodded towards the prisoner. 'I take it you'll be hangin' this fella?'

'As soon as we get a jury together and build a gallows. There ain't a lot we can do until early next week.'

'I guess not. It usually takes a few days to sober

up the judge.'

The two men laughed, and Eli, having pacified his visitor, produced the whiskey.

Phil Jones was practically ignored by his uncle. He poured out coffee for the two men, gave a tin mug of it to the prisoner, and took his own drink out to the porch. There was something puzzling him but he tried to put the suspicions to the back of his mind. He sat on the rickety cane chair and viewed the main street as it lay under the high sun of early afternoon. Flies were buzzing around and the few horses outside the saloon were stirring uneasily while their owners refreshed themselves.

Harry Vernon's hands were still sitting restlessly on their tired animals. They looked enviously at the deputy but were wary about making any comments in his hearing. They knew he was the nephew of their boss, and they had often wondered why he did not play a part in running the Vernon spread.

The rancher emerged about half an hour later. He carried the money-bag in his left hand and passed it up to one of the horsemen. Then he cast a glance at his seated nephew.

'You should be ridin' with these fellas,' he said in an attempt to be friendly. 'You'd be right welcome back at the spread, young fella. It's the future, but if you stay here you'll still be playin' at deputies ten years or more from now.'

'I'm content, Uncle Harry,' Phil said without moving from his seat. 'I ain't no rancher.'

Harry Vernon hesitated before unhitching his cow pony.

'I always got room for another hand,' he said. 'Just remember that, Phil.'

'I'll remember, Uncle Harry.'

The rancher swung into the saddle. 'Let's head for home,' he ordered his escort.

'We're all pretty thirsty, boss,' one of them said bravely. 'It's been a long ride.'

'You have water bottles,' the rancher snapped as he swung his horse round. 'We gotta get this money back to the ranch so that we're there when them bulls arrive. If you fellas start drinkin' in the Golden Bell, none of you will be fit to leave town till the morning. Once we finish this deal and them cattle is safely among our stock, you'll all get a five-dollar bonus and you can come into town for the weekend. Bring Wally and the chuck wagon with you and make a big thing of it.'

The hands cheered up and rode out of town at a brisk pace.

Friday passed quietly and the Elverton folk watched with keen interest the building of a small scaffold at the southern end of the town. The mayor had persuaded twelve of the more sober citizens to form a jury, and the children had been promised a day off school. The court would sit in their large classroom. Phil and the marshal stayed at the jailhouse and Mrs Anderson supplied food and drink. It was on Saturday that things began to go wrong.

Marshal Anderson was still in pain and sat morosely at his desk that morning. The windows of the cells had been boarded up, the back door was provided with an extra bolt, and shotguns still lay on the desk, ready loaded. Phil Jones had gone down to the telegraph office to send off a report to the County Sheriff, and the town seemed quiet.

The prisoner had finished his breakfast and Eli's mind was brought back from his own aches and pains as the man placed his tin plate and mug on the floor. The marshal turned to look at him. The side of the man's face and head were swathed in bandages and his right arm was in a sling. He was unshaven but wore a fresh shirt given him by the marshal. The prisoner had hardly spoken and Eli would normally have given him a sound beating until he got more co-operative. He did not feel able to do it now, and Phil had refused to help.

The marshal got slowly to his feet and went across to the bars.

'Look, fella,' he said in as friendly a manner as he could, manage, 'we got you fair and square on this hold-up business. If the judge has anythin' to do with it, you're for a hangin' some time next week. Somebody tried to kill you the other night. It weren't just some local fella feelin' like revenge. It was the man you came into town to meet. He's as scared as hell you're gonna talk. Why protect him now?'

The prisoner came slowly over to the bars.

'You imagine I ain't thought about that?' he asked. 'You got any lawyers in town?'

The marshal blinked. 'Sure we have. Jesse Maynard is as good a lawyer as you can get. What you figure on doin' with a lawyer? They cost money.'

'I got money. There was fifteen dollars in my poke when you locked me up here. And I got a horse and saddle. So I wanta see that lawyer.'

The marshal sighed. 'Well, I guess you got your rights,' he conceded, 'but what the hell good will it do you?'

The prisoner leaned against the bars until his face was within inches of the metalwork.

'I don't aim to hang if I can prevent it,' he said softly. 'You want to know the name of my contact in Elverton, and I wanta save my neck. We can make a deal, but only with it all written up legal-like. I'll plead guilty to holdin' up the stage but not to killin' the guard. A few shots were fired and any one of us coulda done it. It can't be pinned on me. I'll go to the county jail and take my chances. But I don't want no one goin' back on a promise

42

once I've talked. You savvy?'

Eli nodded.

'I savvy,' he said grimly. 'Folks is gonna be disap-pointed, but we sure want the name of the fella who's sellin' out. I'll speak to Jesse Maynard and to the judge.'

Lawyer Maynard did not work on a Saturday and the marshal called at his home in the early after-noon. The little attorney was reading a book when his wife ushered the lawman into his presence. Eli explained the reason for his visit and the man's little weasel eyes brightened.

'Has he got money?' he asked eagerly.

The marshal told him that he had and the deal was done. Eli returned to the jailhouse to assure the prisoner that the lawyer was anxious to be of help and would be paying a call on Monday morn-ing. But Jesse Maynard had another call to make first. He would be at the Golden Bell on Saturday night with his friends. An appearance in court would be a feather in his cap. He would be making some impassioned plea in front of the whole town. He would be the centre of attention. Jesse Maynard could hardly wait to let his friends know what a key part he was going to play in the most important trial that Elverton had experienced for years.

Saturday night was also the time when the

ranch hands from the Vernon spread came into town. The five men who had escorted Harry had extra money in their pockets, and another three or four would be accompanying them with the chuck wagon hitched and well supplied with food.

They camped outside town, washed themselves to get rid of the worst of the dust, and then headed into Elverton as the sun went down and the lights came on in the windows all along the main street. A few hands from other ranches would meet up with them and the work of the different spreads would be discussed over whiskey and beer.

Saturday was always a busy night for the marshal and his deputy. They normally patrolled the town to discourage too much fighting, but tonight would be different. Both of them had to stay at the jailhouse to watch over their prisoner. Eli Anderson still felt that some attempt might be made either to rescue or kill the man. So he and Phil sat tight behind closed doors and just listened to the growing noise on the main street.

The jailhouse was warm and the coffee smelt strong as the two men sat with their feet on the desk and made sleepy conversation. Eli's arm was still giving him trouble and he moved restlessly in his chair. The prisoner had dozed off, his mouth wide open and his bandages slightly bloodstained and needing replacement. Phil was about to get up and pour some more coffee when there was a loud banging on the door. The two lawmen looked at each other, grabbed shotguns, and waited for some shout to identify the caller.

It was the mayor. His strident voice woke the prisoner, who sat up looking scared under the dim lamplight.

Phil admitted the First Citizen and the stout little man wiped a furrowed brow with a large bandanna.

'We got problems over at the Golden Bell, Eli,' he said breathlessly. 'That damned fool Jesse Maynard has been boastin' to folk about bein' a defence lawyer for this fella here. Folks is real upset and them ranch hands from the Vernon spread are drunk enough to stir up real trouble.'

Eli looked at Phil and went out to the stoop where he could get a good view of the saloon up the street. The place was noisy enough but not much worse than the usual Saturday night.

'Maybe it would quieten down if I went across,' he said uncertainly. He glanced at Phil. 'You keep on your guard here, lad,' he advised. 'It could be that some folks is buildin' up trouble so that we have to leave the jailhouse and give them a chance to get this fella outa here. If anyone tries anythin' on, just blast away and I'll come running.'

The marshal placed a few cartridges in the pocket of his vest and tucked the shotgun under his arm. He knew from experience that his presence would be enough to deter trouble. He was angry with himself for not telling the lawyer to keep his fool mouth shut. The whole town had liked the stage guard and lawyers had few friends among the folk of Elverton. Eli Anderson gave a sigh and went out into the night.

There were a few drunks on the steps of the saloon but they parted respectfully as the marshal passed them. The gun under his arm was enough to give him an air of calm authority. He went through the swing doors and stood beneath the bright light from the large brass-and-copper oil-lamps. There were two groups that seemed to be having separate arguments. He knew some of the people involved but others were ranch hands from neighbouring spreads. Some of the town folk seemed to be quarrelling as well, and the owner was standing on the stairs. He looked uncertain about the outcome.

His face brightened when he saw the marshal, and a sudden silence fell on the warm room as everybody began to realize that the law had arrived. Eli Anderson stood silently for a while. He looked around quietly before advancing to the middle of the floor.

'There's folk in this town tryin' to get some sleep,' he said in an almost conversational voice. 'I know it's Saturday night, but I'd sure be grateful if you'd just keep the noise down. I wouldn't like to get mad at anybody and spoil their looks.'

There was an almost sheepish nodding of heads but one of the local storekeepers had the courage to speak up.

'Folks is sayin' that Jesse Maynard aims to get that killer saved from a hanging,' he shouted. 'What sorta justice is that? That hold-up fella shot Ted Larby and we don't aim to see some crooked lawyer set him loose.'

The marshal sighed as other angry voices were raised.

'Just hold it, fellas,' he said in a louder voice. 'This killer is gonna be tried by Judge Murphy and twelve of you as a jury. That's what courts is all about. Now, all Lawyer Maynard is doin' is to make sure that the fella's treated accordin' to law. He certainly held up the stage, and he'll go to the county jail for ten years or more. But the killin' is bein' argued about. A few shots were fired and there were five fellas in the hold-up. I don't reckon as how we've anythin' to worry about. I figure he'll hang in the end, so just be patient with all this legal double-talk. Don't start makin' trouble around town.'

'Suppose he don't hang?'

Eli Anderson looked at the man who asked the question. He was a tall, slender fellow with a thin face and scant fair hair. The marshal recognized

47

him as one of Harry Vernon's line riders. 'That's for the judge and jury,' he snapped.

The man persisted. 'We're bein' told around town that this fella was tryin' to steal money from my boss. Mr Vernon's a good boss and he deserves justice. We're gonna see he gets it.'

There was a chorus of agreement and the marshal heard some murmuring of lynching the prisoner. He tried to shift the gun under his arm but suddenly realized his dificulty. He could not use his left hand. It was swollen and sore. The splint kept it at an angle and he had to push the barrel of the shotgun forward as best he could with the right arm. It was still going to be hard to cock it, and he began to sweat as some of the men started to move towards the door.

He decided to place the scatter-gun on the nearest table. That gave him a free hand with easy reach to the Colt .44 at his side. He felt more comfortable but things were getting beyond control. Some of the older and more sober customers tried to keep the peace, but the drinkers were more determined to do something.

Eli Anderson drew his gun and pulled back the hammer. He stood between the mob and the door.

'Now, just cool it!' he shouted. 'I ain't havin' no lynchin' in my town. Leave this to the law.'

What happened next was never quite explained. Folks talked about it for weeks afterwards, but nobody agreed. A glass beer-tankard flew across the saloon and hit the marshal in the chest. It shattered when it struck the floor and the noise it made joined in the sound of the shot. Eli Anderson's finger pulled the trigger in a sort of reflex action. A ranch hand staggered backwards and let out a yell. Blood welled from his right forearm and he clutched it in agony.

There was a sudden silence as they all stared at the injured man. The marshal stepped over the broken pieces of glass and spoke to one of the bartenders.

'Go get Doc Harper,' he said in a shaken voice. Then he turned to the rest of the men as they looked at each other with slightly shamed expressions. 'Now you can see where this sorta thing gets you,' he said. 'Let's just settle down and see that nobody else gets hurt. Now, I'm goin' back to the jailhouse, and if I hear one more bit of trouble tonight, I'll be back here again. And my shootin' won't be no accident next time.'

FIVE

Marshal Anderson lay back in the chair with a welcome cup of coffee in his hand. The jailhouse was warm and the prisoner had woken to stand at the bars with a strained expression on his face. There was no doubt what the folk of the town wanted to do to him. He accepted the coffee that Phil gave him with a nervous nod of thanks.

'I think it'll quieten down now,' the marshal said as he tried flexing the fingers of the injured hand. He was in pain and suddenly felt very tired.

'Who was causin' all the trouble?' Phil asked.

'Oh, you couldn't pin it down, but them ranch hands from the Vernon spread was drunk and the locals was real riled at the idea of Lawyer Maynard takin' an interest.' He shook his head. 'I don't blame 'em, but we can't have a lynchin' over this. Things like that unsettle a place and it takes months for folk to look each other in the face again.'

He put down the cup and studied his right hand. It was trembling slightly.

'I think I'm gettin' past this job, Phil.' He sighed. 'You may be marshal sooner than you think.'

The two men grinned at each other and Phil poured more drinks. The town did seem quieter and the loudest noise was the fluttering of insects around the lamps. The prisoner went back to his bunk and the lawmen began to doze in their chairs. Eli Anderson shook himself awake and looked at the clock on the wall.

'I feel real tired out,' he said apologetically. 'I'll go take a couple of hours rest and then you call me so that we can keep watch like we did last night. And don't open that door until you knows who it is.'

Phil nodded and watched his boss retire to the empty cell. He picked up the battered pack of playing-cards and began to lay them out for a game of solitaire. Eli Anderson was soon snoring and the prisoner seemed to be dozing off as well. Phil played for half an hour, listening for every noise floating in from the main street.

He got bored after a while and sat back in the marshal's chair with his feet on the desk. His eyes started to close as the rhythm of the older man's snores began to lull him to sleep.

It was a crash of glass that brought Phil back to sudden reality. He sat up and stared at the door for a moment. He was trying to figure out exactly what had caused the noise. Then it came again. A window was being smashed somewhere on the main street. Phil jumped out of his chair and ran to the shutters. His fingers tore at the bolts as he drew them.

He could see the people up near the saloon and hear their shouting. The windows of the Golden Bell seemed to be intact and the attention of the crowd appeared to be directed at some event further down and across the street. He turned to wake the marshal but found him already scrambling out of the cell and coming to join him at the window.

Eli Anderson strapped on his belt and checked the gun at his side.

'Open up, lad,' he said tersely. 'I'll go settle this and knock a few heads together.'

He made a move towards the door but stopped suddenly and let out a moan. He clutched his left arm and cursed loudly.

'This damned thing is hurtin' like hell,' he said angrily. 'I reckon as how you'd better get out there, lad. Can you handle it?'

'I reckon so,' Phil said with a grin.

'Oh, I know you can shoot better than anybody

else in town, but I don't want no killings. Just calm 'em down and get them off to their beds. It's gone midnight and they won't be in a fightin' mood. Take the scatter-gun. The sight of that should be enough. See whose windows they're smashin' while you're at it. Though I reckon I can guess who ain't the host popular fella in town right now.'

'So can I.' Phil grinned as he picked up the gun.

They opened the front door of the jailhouse and both went out to the boardwalk. The cool breeze hit them as they stared down the street towards a gang of drunks who were gathered outside the building where Lawyer Maynard lived and conducted his business. Even as the lawmen appeared, somebody in the crowd threw another missile. It shattered one of the upper windows and Phil thought he could hear a scream from Ma Maynard.

'Go break 'em up, lad,' the marshal ordered. 'I'll lock this place up again so don't forget to hammer like hell on the door. I'll be in a shootin' mood if anyone else wants to get in.'

'You still think somebody will try gettin' that fella out, Marshal?' Phil asked.

'Either that or try killin' him again. All this hootin' and hollerin' ain't no accident. There's somethin' behind it all. And your Uncle Harry's fellas bein' in town with the other ranch hands, ain't gonna help to keep the peace.'

Phil tucked the shotgun under his arm and began walking down the street. He heard the bolts slamming home on the jailhouse door and bit his lips as he realized that he was now alone.

The visiting ranch hands were playing little part in what was happening. They were all gathered outside the saloon watching the locals. Phil knew most of the people involved and did not relish having to take a tough line with them. He walked slowly down the street and placed himself between the crowd and the building they were attacking. A sudden hush fell on the town.

The deputy marshal looked hard at one of the young livery-stable lads who was holding a piece of broken horseshoe in his hand.

'If you throw that, Lem,' the lawman said firmly, 'I'll be givin' you a bed in the jailhouse. So drop it.'

The youth stared back for a moment, then the silent crowd heard the missile clatter to the ground.

'Now suppose you all go home. You've had a good night out, and it don't become grown men to go frightenin' women in their own homes.'

There was a wave of muttering and the crowd began to thin as some of them realized what they had been doing in the heat of the moment. But one of the younger lads still held a missile in his drunken grip. As a final gesture of defiance, he hurled it at the home of the hated lawyer and had the pleasure of hearing another window shatter on impact.

What happened next took them all by surprise. The blast of a shotgun deafened the ears. The flash came from an upper window that was already broken. Another blast followed and some of the crowd recoiled as buckshot peppered them amid shouts of anger and pain. Then a figure appeared at the window. It was Ma Maynard.

'You killed my man!' she shrieked down at them. 'He's lyin' dead back there and the folk of this town have killed him.'

There was a sudden hush. The injured men were forgotten and everyone stared at the frantic figure at the window. When she burst into loud sobs, the crowd began to disperse and the doctor suddenly appeared, carrying his bag. Either he had heard the shooting or somebody had knocked on his door. He hurried into the building while Phil stood undecided for a moment.

The ranch hands were going shamefacedly back into the saloon while other folk were seeking their homes in the hope that nobody would remember the part they had played in all the trouble. Phil decided to follow the doctor and entered the office of Lawyer Maynard. No lights were on and glass crunched under his feet. He followed the medical man through to the stairs and up to the living-quarters.

Jesse Maynard was in the bedroom. He lay at the side of the large bed, his collar loosened and his face contorted with pain. Doc Harper bent over him while a distraught Mrs Maynard looked on.

'Heart attack,' the medical man eventually announced. 'All this uproar was too much for him. I'd had him under treatment for the past year.'

The mayor suddenly appeared in the doorway. He had watched from the shelter of his own building until he felt it safe to play the concerned friend. He put an arm round Ma Maynard and mumbled as many platitudes as he could command. Phil Jones felt out of place and decided to go back to the jailhouse. There was nothing he could do and he was sick of the whole business.

He left the building and was glad to breathe the fresh air again. The town was quiet now and even the saloon seemed to be subdued. He walked slowly back to the jailhouse and knocked on the heavy door with the butt of the shotgun.

'It's Phil Jones, Marshal,' he bawled. 'It's all quieted down now but I sure as hell got some bad news to deliver.'

He waited patiently but nothing happened. Another banging with the scatter-gun produced no result. Phil went to one of the shuttered windows and tried to peep through the tiny gaps into the lighted office beyond. He could not see any movement. He was just about to shout again when he was joined by the mayor.

'I'll lay odds that he's gone fast asleep,' the First Citizen growled as he hammered with his fists and called out his own name.

There was still no response and the two men looked at each other.

'I'll go round the back,' Phil said quietly.

He was worried now. Eli Anderson was not a man to go to sleep at such a time, and the young deputy hurried round the side of the building. The rear door was also locked and he banged on it to echo the noise the mayor was making round at the front. There was still no answer. He went back to join the mayor.

A few people were gathering now and the blacksmith appeared with a large hammer.

'You want I should break in?' he asked.

'I reckon as how you'd better,' the mayor said anxiously. 'There's somethin' sure as hell wrong in there.'

The sledge-hammer struck the door with several resounding crashes. The wood shattered and it sprang open to let out a stream of light onto the dark stoop. They crowded in and stopped in stunned surprise at the sight in front of them.

57

The two cells were empty and Marshal Anderson lay on the floor by his desk. Blood encircled his head and his gun was still in the holster.

SIX

Mayor Raynor's office was above his dry-goods store. He had a prosperous business. It was run mainly by his rotund wife and two skinny daughters. The young girls were still unmarried and seemed doomed to spend their lives behind the counter. Their mama did not consider any of the local lads good enough for them and the mayor did not want to have to employ staff who would demand wages.

His office was full of cigar smoke as he and the five councilmen sat around the large desk. The First Citizen had never called a meeting so early in the day, and for that reason there was no welcoming whiskey for the small group of visitors.

'Now, I'll lay it on the line, fellas,' he said by way of introduction. 'Last night was one hell of a disaster. We had all them drunk ranch hands in town and some folk took advantage of it to get that prisoner outa jail. The doc here tells me that Marshal Anderson was hit across the head with what coulda been the butt of a gun. Whoever did it was let into the jail' – he looked round the room – 'and that means that it was somebody he knew and trusted.'

The judge blew out a cloud of smoke and let some ash drop on to his waistcoat. 'Eli Anderson was a cautious man,' he said slowly. 'He knew that there might be an attempt to free the prisoner, so he'd be mighty careful. It wasn't no stranger, and that means that we're lookin' for somebody close to home.'

There was a nodding of heads and Doctor Harper cleared his throat.

'Eli didn't even reach for his gun,' he said quietly. 'He seems to have opened the back door and let somebody in. The blow was struck from the rear and killed him just about instantly. Real powerful, it were.'

There was a slight silence before the mayor continued.

'So now we have to decide on a new marshal,' he said as he looked round the office.

It was the judge who spoke.

'Phil Jones is a bright lad,' he said. 'Better than most and as honest as we could wish. Make him the marshal.'

There was a murmur of agreement but the mayor leaned forward across the desk as though imparting some great truth.

'We got ourselves a problem there,' he said solemnly. 'Young Phil is too close to his Uncle Harry Vernon. Now, I ain't sayin' as how the lad is influenced by the old goat, but kin is kin, and Harry has got troubles right now that could place young Phil on the spot.'

'You mean this rustlin' thing?' the livery-stable owner asked.

'Exactly. Harry wanted me to have Eli Anderson or his deputy chasin' all over the territory lookin' for the folk what is doin' the rustlin' round here. We got a town to run, and I figure what happened last night is a clear sign that we sure as hell can't have lawmen gallopin' around the countryside while the ranchers have men of their own to do their dirty work. Phil might feel under an obligation to his uncle, and I don't aim to put him to the test. We gotta have an older marshal. Somebody who's got maturity and puts the town first. I think we're all agreed on that.'

'Who you got in mind?' the judge asked cynically amid the nodding of heads.

The mayor shuffled in his seat under the judge's hard gaze.

'Well, I was thinkin' of Ed Welsey,' he said. 'He's good with a gun, as honest as any man can be, and he's level-headed.'

'And he's your kin,' the judge murmured.

'That don't matter,' the mayor snapped back. 'We all live right here in town, and not out there back of beyond. Ed will work for Elverton, not for the ranchers who just use our town when it suits them.'

One of the storekeepers ventured to interrupt. They all turned to look at him.

'We ain't aimin' to upset the ranchers, I hope?' he murmured. 'They spend big money here. Elverton needs them.'

He had hit on an important point and the next few minutes passed in discussing the financial plight that would be created if the ranchers took their business elsewhere. Then one of the store-owners brought up another matter.

'And we ain't got a lawyer no more,' he pointed out. 'We might not like the fellas but we sure need 'em now and then.'

They all looked at the judge and he gave a modest grin.

'I ain't practised law for many a year,' he admitted, 'and bein' a judge has made me a bit rusty on drawin' up contracts and wills, I guess. But I'll help out until some bright young fella comes along.'

They all agreed and the meeting began to break up. Only the judge stayed behind, and after a quick glance at the wall clock, the mayor decided it was time to break out the whiskey. The judge sipped gratefully and sprawled in his chair.

'So what's young Phil Jones gonna think of all this?' he asked.

'Well, he's a young fella who's got more money than most,' Bert Raynor said after a moment's thought. 'His ma and pa left him that hotel in Phoenix and that must bring in a few dollars a week. I always reckon the law job is just a way of makin' himself useful.'

'He don't seem to want to work for his Uncle Harry.'

'Would you? That old rogue ain't the sort to appeal to an honest young fella. And Phil did once say that he never had a yen to be a-herdin' cattle in every sorta weather. No, I figure as how he'll accept the situation. Maybe even prefer it. After all, the deputy don't get the blame when things go wrong.'

The judge grunted and held out his empty glass.

'And where is our local hero right now?' he asked.

'He's tailin' them fellas that freed the prisoner. I don't reckon as how it will come to anythin' with the sorta wind that's been blowin' all night. But we had to show willin' or folks would talk. There were signs of horses back of the jailhouse. They might just lead somewhere.'

Judge Murphy got up from his chair and

stretched himself.

'Well, we got quite a week ahead of us,' he said wearily. 'Two funerals and a new marshal. Elverton don't get that much excitement very often. Just make sure that damn-fool preacher don't go on too long about the goodness of the Almighty. I don't see a lot of it about.'

'Things will be back to normal in a day or two, and then you'll be complainin' about how dull the place is.'

'I reckon you're right. When you get to my age, Elverton seems like the waitin' room to eternity.'

Phil Jones had ridden out on the trail of the jail-house raiders early that morning. Nothing could have been done till daylight and he felt that he was wasting his time anyway. The westerly wind had scoured the ground during the night. It still blew the dust in waist-high gusts and any marks on the dry earth would soon vanish.

The young deputy had quite a few thoughts about the happenings in town. As the late marshal had said, everything seemed to have had some sort of planning behind it and the two lawmen had fallen into the trap. A bit of apparently drunken talk in the saloon would have been enough to set the wilder elements alight. Lawyer Maynard had made it worse by his boasting.

Phil checked at the back of the jailhouse as

soon as the morning sky was bright enough. As the mayor had told the judge, there were still signs of several horses and he found the jail keys lying on the stoop where the killer had dropped them after locking up as he left. Nothing in the building had helped, and all the young deputy could do was to use his commonsense in following a vanishing trail.

The few tracks that the wind had left pointed due south. Phil set out in that direction. He picked up an occasional sign that told him he was going the right way. It was reasonable to suppose that the group was heading for the border. A journey west or north would have taken them through land owned by the big ranchers. That would be risky. Then there was the question of watering their horses. They had to head towards a creek of some sort before the animals let them down.

Tillburn Creek was the likeliest target. The barely marked trail was leading in that direction and Phil was reasonably sure that he had made the right decision. He rode slowly under the increasing heat of the day, trying to forget about what had happened back in the jailhouse and concentrate on what his own problems would be when he met up with the killers. It would take about four hours of riding before he could hope to reach the creek. It had been a few years since he had been there; the trail was seldom used and badly grown over. The few hoof-marks left by the raiders were also fading away and Phil had to do a certain amount of guessing that he was on the right track.

It was late afternoon when he spotted some familiar landmarks. He breathed a sigh of relief as he topped a rise and saw the thin flow of water amid a group of trees. His horse smelt it and hastened the pace to quench its thirst. It bore down on the creek without any guidance from the rider. Phil let the animal drink while he stared around at the lush grass that grew along the edges of the creek. There was some flattening and a few hoof-marks had survived in the damper parts. The young deputy had guessed right and he dismounted to investigate more closely.

Elverton was a very subdued place when Marshal Anderson was laid to rest in the burial plot behind the meeting-hall. The whole town seemed to have turned out for the event. Even a few of the big ranchers had ridden in to pay their respects. The preacher cut his sermonizing shorter than usual. It might have been due to a hint from the mayor or the fact that he had the lawyer's funeral to conduct an hour later.

Jesse Maynard was not as popular as the marshal. Fewer people turned out, and the widow was still prostrated in her bedroom behind the newly glazed windows of their home.

Harry Vernon retired to the saloon after the marshal's burial service. Three other ranchers joined him and they all drank silently until it was time for their meeting with the mayor.

Bert Raynor was not looking forward to the meeting. He eyed the four men anxiously as they took seats in his office and refused the soothing glasses of whiskey that he offered. That was a bad sign in itself.

'You fellas seem to have somethin' on your minds,' he said with an attempt at light-heartedness. Their faces did not change expression. It was old Harry Vernon who acted as spokesman.

'This ain't a social call, Bert,' he said grimly. 'We ranchers made this town. Without us, you'd be the mayor of a few wooden shacks and a privy. We've just been checkin' on our cattle, and I reckon that a thousand head of good beef stock has gone missin' in the last coupla weeks. You gotta do somethin' about it.'

The mayor had expected something like this and he spread his hands in a gesture of despair.

'What the hell can I do?' he pleaded. 'You've just been to Eli's burial and you already know that young Phil is out in the wilds tryin' to get a lead on the fellas involved. I ain't got no more lawmen in Elverton. And even if I had, what the hell could they do? Your ranches cover half the territory, and between you all you must have forty or fifty riders

67

who know the land much better than any town fella can.'

He looked at the four men and his eyes flickered nervously for a moment.

'And what about Lars Peterson?' he asked. 'Why ain't he with you? Or ain't he losin' any cattle?'

The four ranchers were silent for a moment. Then it was Art Rubin who spoke up. He was a short, thickset man with dark face and greying, thick hair.

'I sent one of my boys over to his place the other day,' he said. 'He ain't had no problems.'

'I reckon he puts that down to havin' the Almighty on his side,' Vic Lawrence said unkindly. He was a tall, thin man with a crooked mouth that moved constantly as he chewed tobacco.

'That psalm-singin' old devil must be the only rancher within miles who ain't been bothered by these rustlers,' Harry Vernon said thoughtfully. 'I calls that mighty strange.'

'Maybe he just keeps a careful eye on his stock,' the mayor suggested.

'Well, he certainly don't pasture any of his animals with our brands,' Art Rubin said. 'Seems to take some sorta pleasure in not mixin' with his neighbours.'

'We ain't good enough for him,' said Harry. He scratched his chin thoughtfully. 'But now that you've brung up the matter, it is strange that he ain't been bothered. He's got some good stock down Foley Canyon way.'

He leaned across the desk to make sure that he had the mayor's full attention.

'Now, I'm gonna put it to you straight, Bert,' he said in a low, determined voice. 'Us ranchers is gettin' just a bit tired of this thievin' that's goin' on. The law's gotta do somethin' about it. Our hands are not gunfighters. You gotta give us a little help. Take on more deputies. Pay out posse money. Call in the military if necessary. And at least get on to the territory politicos and have the county do somethin' as well. If you don't get off your ass, Bert, we'll be doin' our buyin' and our drinkin' some place else.'

The mayor swallowed noisily. 'I'll call a council meetin' first thing tomorrow,' he promised. 'I've already appointed a new marshal and Phil will probably be back here in the morning. Just give me time to get things organized.'

Harry Vernon got to his feet and the other three ranchers followed suit.

'Well, I'll be callin' on you tomorrow,' Harry said bluntly. 'I'm stayin' in town tonight because I got me some business at the bank. These fellas is leavin' for home. They have further to travel than I have. So I'll send riders off to tell them what your council decides. I'll wish you a good day, Bert, and don't forget to tell these council fellas that we ain't

THE VERNON BRAND

foolin' around. This is costin' us money.'

The mayor nodded despondently and saw the ranchers to the front of the building.

'You're stayin' at the hotel, Harry?' he asked.

'And pay their fancy prices?' The rancher snorted. 'Like hell I am. I've got Wally Payne and the chuck wagon on the edge of town. A better bed and better food than anythin' the hotel can manage.'

He turned to leave and then stopped as a thought struck him.

'What does young Phil think about not bein' the new marshal?' he asked sharply.

The mayor licked his lips. 'Well, the council didn't feel that he was old enough for the job,' he said hesitantly. 'Nothin' personal against the young fella, but marshallin' needs an older man. Gives the folk more confidence.'

'So who gets the job?'

'Ed Welsey.'

The words were spoken softly and the mayor was surprised when old Harry's face broke into a broad grin.

'You sure knows how to look after the town's best interests,' he said with delicate sarcasm, 'and you just done me one hell of a favour. I gotta thank you for that, Bert.'

'You're pleased?' The mayor could not conceal his surprise.

70

'I sure am. That young fella's got his pride. We're a mighty proud family. When he comes back to town and you break the news to him, you'll have lost a deputy. I'll have gained the best shot and best brain in the territory. I'll see you tomorrow, Bert. After your council meeting.'

He waved a hand in farewell and hurried after the other ranchers.

When Harry Vernon returned to the mayoral office the next day his nephew was there. Phil Jones had got back from trailing the raiders and had just finished his report when Harry arrived. The rancher greeted his nephew with a nod and sat down opposite the mayor. The young deputy was left standing as befitted his position.

'So how did your council meeting go?' the rancher asked. 'I hope you put it to them plainly.'

'Oh, I did, Harry, I sure did,' the mayor assured him.

He then went on to make as many promises as he could that the ranchers would receive full co-operation from Elverton. Both men knew that the political gestures were not quite all they appeared to be, but Harry listened patiently. Phil just stood silently and was not even offered a glass of whiskey. He had already been told of the man appointed over his head and was studying his uncle and the mayor with a new interest. A very personal interest.

When Bert Raynor had finished speaking, he mopped his brow and waited for the rancher to comment on what he had said. Harry Vernon glanced at his nephew and put the empty glass down on the desk.

'Promises are easy things,' he said slowly. 'Now, I ain't callin' you a liar, Bert, but you is in politics. I want some real action, and I don't aim to go back to the other ranchers and tell 'em that I've been left without a deal.'

The mayor shifted uneasily in his chair and then leaned forward as though confiding some great secret.

'I'll let you have young Phil here for four weeks,' he said. 'The council don't like it but I stood up to them. Phil can back-trail all them rustlin' fellas north as far as the cattle pens at the railhead. They have to sell them some place. He can ask questions there and find out if any cattle with local brands have been offered for sale. How does that sound?'

Harry Vernon blinked in surprise and looked hard at his nephew.

'I didn't think you'd be stayin' on as a deputy, young fella,' he said reproachfully. 'Ain't you got no pride?'

'I got pride, Uncle Harry,' Phil said quietly, 'but I'm still young, and when things go wrong in a town, I'd rather not be the one takin' the blame.

I'm only the deputy.'

'I told you he was a wise one,' the mayor said proudly, 'and we got some information for you, Harry. About that prisoner that was broke out of the jailhouse. You'll be interested.'

Harry Vernon stood up to go. He appeared angry that his plans for Phil were not working out. Taking the young man back to the ranch would have been a major triumph.

'Not interested in them hold-up fellas,' he said sourly. 'It would have been a good thing to know who gave the information to them, but it's over and done with now.'

'Not quite.' The mayor's voice was suddenly confident and the rancher paused on his way to the door.

'Go on,' Harry said as he glanced at the two men.

'Tell him, Phil,' the mayor prompted the young deputy.

'I managed to follow the trail as far as Tillburn Creek,' the deputy said quietly. 'It faded out beyond that point. The wind had covered all the tracks. But they'd stopped to rest the horses and cook some food. Lit a fire, they did, and I found some of the paper they used to light it.'

Phil took a small envelope from his shirt pocket and emptied the contents on to the desk. There were several pieces of charred paper. Printing could be seen and Harry picked one of the scraps up and took it over to the window.

'Some sorta prayer-book,' he said slowly. 'So what the hell? They just used it to get the fire goin' is all.'

The mayor smiled. 'But who owned the prayer-book, Harry?' he crowed. 'I supplied them prayer-books from this very store five or six years back. Twenty-five of the things with nice red bindings and bookmarks of coloured silk. The fella what bought them was a God-botherin' rancher who wanted to be sure that all his people had the word of the Almighty to hand every minute of the day. And the same fella ain't had no cattle rustled. How's that for a find? You can't say now that this town ain't out to help you.'

SEVEN

Ross Logan wiped the sweat from his brow and looked longingly at the doors of the saloon. He was loading supplies on to the one-mule wagon and the day was getting hotter as the sun reached its zenith. He heaved the last sack of flour into position, wiped his hands on already dusty pants, and went off determinedly in the direction of the Golden Bell.

Working for a rancher like Lars Peterson was not easy. The consumption of alcohol was frowned upon and the boss was never slow at delivering a lecture on the evils of drink. But today was different. Ross was alone in town and nobody was around to carry tales. He had a few dollars in his pocket and could afford a decent meal and a few drinks before taking the two-day journey back to the Peterson spread.

He had already noticed that old Harry Vernon

was in town. His chuck wagon was at the side of the trail and Wally Payne was driving the rancher and cooking his food. Wally had been around for as long as Ross could remember and was already in the Golden Bell enjoying the fruits of his labour. Ross was determined to join him.

It was an hour or more later when he rolled out of the saloon to put the feed-bag on his patient mule before wandering down to Belle's Restaurant for a cheap meal. He would sleep on the wagon for the night, but plenty of drink and a hot stew would make it all the more comfortable.

Belle's Restaurant was just behind the main street. The corrals of the local horse-dealer had to be passed to reach it. Ross Logan remembered that there was something he had to check on. He stopped at the fence and peered owlishly at the ponies that stood by the water-trough. There were a couple of mules with them and they all looked without interest at the whiskey-breathed man who was staring at them.

Ross let out a sudden gasp of anger and went along to the gate. He swung it open and entered the corral. The horses paid more attention now and it took him a few noisy minutes before he managed to get his hand on the halter of the one he wanted. He began to lead it from the corral.

The noise had attracted the horse-dealer. He came out of a nearby barn and took in the situation at a glance. Reg Strode was a short, stocky man with a taut, watchful face and uncertain temper. He was getting on to his sixties but looked younger with his flat stomach and well-muscled appearance.

'What the hell is you playin' at, fella?' he bawled at the intruder.

'I'm takin' back what's been stole,' Ross Logan shouted back. 'I was told that one of my boss's horses was here, and this is the one. It's goin' right back to the Peterson spread.'

'Like hell it is!' the dealer shouted as his hand went down to the gun at his side. 'I ain't given to rustlin' no horses and that one is bein' sold on the orders of Marshal Anderson. So just get your thievin' hands off'n it and shift the hell outer here while you still can.'

Reg Strode drew his Colt as he spoke the words. He pulled back the hammer and fired as Ross Logan reached for his own gun. Ross's .44 was barely clear of the holster when the shot took him in the chest. He staggered against the animal he was holding and tried to raise the pistol. The horse shied at the noise and Ross Logan lost his grasp on the halter. He spun round and slowly sank to the ground as the animal moved clear. There was a moment of silence as Reg Strode looked down on him in almost dazed surprise. Folk began to gather, and one or two who had seen what was happening from afar soon started to tell the others. There was no sympathy for the ranch hand. Reg Strode was considered an honest man and was well established in Elverton.

Old Wally Payne was soon on the scene. His slightly bowed figure was well known to the locals. They stepped aside to let him through. His bearded and sweaty face was full of concern as he knelt at the side of the stricken man and lifted the drooping head.

'He's in a bad way,' he said urgently. 'Help me carry him to Doc Harper's place.'

Several of the onlookers obliged and the injured man was rushed on to the main street and down towards the house of the medical man.

The mayor soon arrived with his new marshal and a rather uninterested Phil Jones trailing behind them. Harry Vernon also put in an appearance and the tale was told about the horse.

'It was the one that was ridden by that fella what ended up in the jailhouse,' Reg Strode explained. 'Marshal Anderson ordered it to be sold. The saddle is at the livery stable so I reckon Eddy Farren has the same orders.' He turned to Phil Jones. 'This fella comes along and accuses me of stealin' it. You know that ain't the case, Phil.'

The young deputy nodded agreement. 'That's true enough,' he said. 'We tried to read the brand but it was overgrown. I reckon that it must have

78

been stolen from the Peterson spread by the fellas what held up the stage.'

Phil went into the corral as the crowd began to disperse. He looked at the horse concerned, ran a hand over its flank, and left the corral with a thoughtful look on his face.

Harry Vernon accompanied the mayor along to the home of Doctor Harper. The wounded man was now lying on the surgery table, and as they arrived, the doctor's wife covered the body with a sheet.

'Ain't nothin' we could do,' she said to the newcomers. 'Old Lars Peterson ain't gonna like this. He hates for his men to get into gunfights, and he'll be firin' off sermons about the iniquities of Elverton.'

'Well, it ain't any fault of ours,' the mayor snorted. 'He should consider himself lucky to get the horse back.'

Mrs Harper was emptying the dead man's pockets. She had already removed the gunbelt and it lay on a side table. To it were now added a few dollars, a wad of chewing tobacco, and the usual little prayer-book that all Lars Peterson's men were supposed to carry. It was a worn little thing that Phil picked up to examine.

It fell open easily to display a gap in the pages. At least half a dozen were missing. They had been roughly torn out and some of the stitched lining had been exposed. Phil showed the little book to the mayor without comment. Bert Raynor raised his eyebrows as he stared at the evidence.

'Let's see them scraps of burnt paper you picked up, Phil,' he said quietly as he held out his hand.

The young deputy passed them over while everybody in the surgery crowded round. The dead man on the table was now forgotten as interest shifted to the little prayer-book. The torn pieces of charred paper seemed to match and the mayor shook his head sadly. He looked at Harry Vernon as the old rancher took the items out of the mayoral hands and examined them for himself.

'It don't make sense,' he murmured unbelievingly. 'Lars Peterson ain't the sort to be mixed up in any shady business. And how in hell would he know about the money I was bringin' into town?'

They started discussing the situation while the doctor poured out some whiskey for his friends. The hired hands who had brought in the dying man left for the saloon. They were not included in the select throng of upright citizens. Phil Jones left with them. He wanted to get some rest and think about his next moves. He escorted Wally Payne as far as the Golden Bell. The old man took Phil by the arm before they parted.

'Your uncle needs you back at the ranch, lad,'

he said urgently. 'Them two lads is no use if Harry takes ill. He talks to me, and I'm tellin' you, fella, he's sure worried about the future of the H bar V.'

Phil looked hard at the old-timer. He had always seemed to be about. He remembered Wally talking to him of cattle breeding, helping him manage his first pony, and teaching him to shoot. But Phil's father and mother were never happy on the Vernon spread. They had moved to Phoenix where life was easier. There was a vague story that Wally might even be part of the family. Grandpa Vernon was reckoned to be quite a fellow with the ladies. Phil had always thought of Wally as an uncle in the old days. It now seemed like another world.

'I don't get on with Uncle Harry,' he said quietly. 'And ranchin' ain't really for me.'

'It's part of your inheritance, lad,' the old man urged. 'You got a share in the spread when Harry goes. Them two sons of his will ruin it for all of us.'

'Well, what could I do? They'd always be outvotin' me.'

'Lookit, Phil, you just got yourself insulted in this town. That crooked mayor has made his own kin the new marshal. You and Eli Anderson was honest lawmen. Folk respected you. Now it's all changed. You gotta take your orders from the mayor and Ed Welsey. The folk will lose all respect for you. Leave while the goin's good. It's the best

81

thing to do. Come to the ranch and help us stop this rustlin' business.'

'I've been ordered to ride north to the railhead and see if I can find any trace of sales up there,' Phil said. 'It's all the town can do.'

'Lookit, Phil,' the old man said urgently, 'Lars Peterson is behind all this. I'll swear to it. Your Uncle Harry won't heed me, but Peterson ain't had no cattle stolen, and now he seems to be back of this stage business. Now, that ain't right. When the other ranchers hear about what happened tonight, they're gonna go hell-bent wild. There'll be a range war and they'll drive the Petersons outa the territory. You can't blame them, but your uncle won't take sides. That ain't gonna make him popular.'

'Wally, no town marshal can stop a range war, and the mayor ain't anxious to have the big ranchers fallin' out with Elverton. The town needs their business. I'll do the best I can, but there's more to this than I can figure right now. Just let me do what I've been ordered to do. Just let's see what I can find out before we start gettin' all fired up.'

'Yeah, I heard tell as how you're bein' sent to the railhead,' the old man snorted. 'One hell of a lotta good that will do. If cattle have been sent East, the fellas what sold them ain't gonna hang around waitin' for you. And there are so many crooked dealers at the pens that you'll likely get shot up for askin' too many questions. It's all a waste of time. I reckon we should make up one big posse and go chase Lars Peterson back wherever he came from. The other ranchers could sure as hell use his land for their own cattle.'

'Let's just play it all legal, Wally,' Phil said calmly. 'I'm settin' out in the mornin' to see what information I can pick up.'

They parted company and the young deputy walked back to the jailhouse. He hesitated outside the telegraph office and almost entered the building. He had a message to send, but Elverton was as leaky as a dried-out barrel.

Somebody important was controlling events, and Phil had the distinct feeling that he, as well as other folk, was being used as part of some intricate plan.

EIGHT

Phil Jones was up and about early the next morning. The new marshal was very agreeable to him leaving on the trip north. The mayor had told his nephew that getting Phil out of the way was only the first step to removing him from his job as deputy. He was willingly lent a mule for carrying his gear and was soon on his way up the main street, heading for the distant railhead.

He was surprised to catch sight of old Wally Payne leaning on the rail outside the bank. The chuck wagon and the mules were alongside and the animals ducked their heads up and down as they explored their feed bags. Phil stopped and greeted the cook of the H bar V ranch.

'You're around early, Wally,' he said. 'And hangin' around the front of a bank, too. I'd figure as how you was gettin' ready to stage a hold-up if I didn't know better.'

The old man grinned and spat out a long jet of tobacco juice.

'I could sure as hell use the money,' he cackled, 'but I'm just waitin' for your Uncle Harry. He's in there with that money-lendin' fella.'

Phil blinked and looked at the windows of the building. There was a light on behind the frosted glass and he frowned in puzzlement.

'It's a bit early for Banker Halliday to be doin' business, ain't it?' he asked.

'Your Uncle Harry's one important man around these parts,' Wally grinned, 'and right now he's on his way to bein' the biggest rancher in the territory. You should be helpin' him, young fella,'

'I'm doin' just that. I'm on my way to the railhead.'

'I reckon as how that's a waste of time. Headin' for Peterson's spread and haulin' the old bastard into town would be more likely to get results. He's behind all this, even if Harry can't see it.'

'We got no proof, except them pages from the prayer-book. It's not enough, Wally.'

'Just take at least one bit of advice. Don't cross Lars Peterson's land. You might never get to the railhead.'

The door of the bank opened and the two men turned their attention to the appearance of Harry Vernon. He came out with a wide grin on his face and greeted his nephew with a wave.

'So you're off on your hunt for them rustlers,' he said as he came down the wooden steps. 'I suppose Wally here has been poisonin' your mind against Lars Peterson.'

Phil nodded. 'He has,' he said, 'but as I told him, them bits of paper don't prove Mr Peterson was behind the rustlin' of your cattle. It just means that some of his men might have been involved. Or that somebody picked up one of them prayer-books that he passes out to his hands. And we can't ask Ross Logan about it. He's dead. You're doin' your bankin' a bit early in the day, Uncle Harry. I've never known Mr Halliday open his doors this time of the morning.'

The old rancher sniffed. 'Where money's concerned, lad, these fellas will do what's needed.'

He took his nephew by the arm and gripped tightly.

'Les Weldon and me has exchanged a few words about the future. He's got no sons and is willin' to sell his spread. We're doin' a deal and I've just raised a loan to buy him out. He's had enough of this rustlin' business. Just think of it, Phil. All that extra land and stock along with my new stud bulls. We'll be the kings of the business. And you're in on it whenever you say the word.'

Phil looked at the sly, watery eyes of his uncle

and eased his arm from the tight grip.

'That money that was on its way from Phoenix,' he said slowly. 'How did you come by that?'

The sly eyes shifted their gaze and the rancher hesitated for a moment.

'Well, since we're all kin,' Harry Vernon said with a disarming grin, 'I can tell you that I raised the money on your hotel. You've nothin' to worry about, son. It's all drawn up real proper by a lawyer. You still own the place and the manager will still be paying money into your bank, all regular-like.'

'You're one slimy old dealer, Uncle Harry,' Phil said with a slight grin. It was exactly as he had expected and he was saved an expensive telegraph messsage to Phoenix.

'I sure am,' the rancher happily agreed. 'That's why I want you with me, lad. We got places to go.'

'With your way of runnin' things, the county jail could be one of them.'

Wally Payne cackled with laughter and went to take the feed-bags off the mules.

'Now, before you leave town, lad,' Harry went on, 'I've got me a little present for you. That old Winchester you have there has seen better days. Let's go across to Feldman's store. He's got a real fine new one that I want you to have. My way of sayin' thanks for the loan, and a good shot needs a good gun.'

Despite Phil's feeble protest, the rancher steered him across to the gunsmith's brick building at the far end of the street. Wally followed on with the chuck wagon and all three men entered the store. Hans Feldman was a stout and cheerful man with a fierce German accent. He greeted the ranch owner with a broad smile and shook hands in his ceremonious fashion. The gun was produced and Phil worked the action lovingly. It was the 1886 model; the very latest of Winchester's products and he did not spurn his uncle's generosity.

'That's sure a fine weapon, Uncle Harry,' he said as he tried the smooth action again.

'It's a .50 calibre, lad, and just my way of sayin' thanks for the loan,' the rancher assured him.

Hans Feldman smiled benevolently as the money was handed over and was even more pleased when Harry bought some ammunition of various calibres.

'You are men I like to deal with,' the gunsmith said happily. 'Men who give this town their business and show their friendship. That is a good thing. There are some who buy their guns in other towns. They treat us with contempt and I spit on them.'

Old Wally put down the shotgun he was examining.

'Who would that be?' he asked.

The gunsmith looked around as if others might overhear although the store was empty of other customers.

'That psalm-singing Peterson fellow,' he said in his guttural voice. 'Two cases of carbines he has had sent from Tombstone. I ask you, is that the way to treat local folk? I would have given him a good price on such a big order.'

Phil put down his newly acquired carbine.

'When did this happen, Mr Feldman?' he asked quietly.

'This very last week. They arrived on the freight wagon and are over at the Wells Fargo office waiting to be picked up. We are talking of big money. Five hundred dollars or more if those cases are full. That is not friendly to our town.'

Harry Vernon looked at Wally and at Phil.

'What the hell would he want a load of carbines for?' he asked. The question was on all their minds and there was a moment of silence.

'I told you he was behind all this,' Wally growled. 'We gotta do somethin' about it, Harry. That connivin' old coot is plannin' some real big trouble.'

'Let's not get too stirred up,' Phil cautioned. 'We'll go across the street to the Wells Fargo office and take a look at these cases.'

The three men left the gunstore and hurried down the main street. The town was getting busier now as the children went off unhappily to school and the other stores began to open their doors.

Vic Dyson was behind the counter at the Wells Fargo office. He was supping a mug of coffee and put down the steaming liquid at the prospect of customers. Phil told him what they had called about and the clerk took them behind the counter to show the two long wooden cases that would hold a dozen carbines each.

'Let's have them opened up,' Wally growled.

'You can't do that,' the Wells Fargo man protested. 'We ain't got no rights to open goods addressed to other folks. These cases is labelled for Mr Peterson of the Double L spread. He's the only one who can bust them open.'

Wally was not in a mood to be deterred. He pushed the elderly clerk out of the way and aimed carefully with the heel of one of his heavy boots. The thin panel gave way and he was able to put his fingers into the gap and prise open the edge of the crate. The wooden shavings were soon removed and Wally pulled out the first of the twelve carbines. It was a Winchester .73 model and he waved it in triumph.

'What did I tell you?' he crowed. 'We gotta let folks know about this, Harry. The other ranchers is entitled to find out what Peterson intends to do with all these guns. And I reckon that new marshal you got should be told as well. That's your job, young Phil.'

Without waiting to argue the matter, Wally threw down the gun and hurried from the office.

'It'll be all round town in ten minutes,' Harry Vernon said sadly. 'Wally's been wantin' somethin' like this to happen. What do you think, Phil?'

'Somethin' big is certainly bein' planned,' the young deputy said slowly.

He apologized to Vic Dyson for what had happened and ushered his uncle out of the office.

'I'll go have a word with our new marshal,' he told Harry Vernon, 'and then I'll be on my way before he gets any new ideas. You'll need to keep Wally in check, Uncle Harry. Those guns could really start trouble if word gets out to the other ranchers. Nobody likes Lars Peterson and they're all spoilin' for a fight.'

Harry nodded. 'Yeah, I reckon as how you're right, Phil. It might be better if you didn't leave town, but I reckon you got your orders. So look after yourself, lad, and don't go doin' nothin' foolish. These rustler fellas are a gang, and you'll be on your own. Get back here safely and come work with me out at the ranch. Leave Elverton to be robbed blind by the mayor and his nephew.'

They parted a few minutes later, Phil to report

to the new marshal before heading north, and Harry Vernon to catch up with a talkative Wally Payne.

NINE

Elverton seethed with the latest gossip. Lars Peterson was bringing in guns to start a range war. Folk saw the weapons being moved from the Wells Fargo office to the safety of the jailhouse. It made for an uneasy atmosphere in the little town. The store owners and the saloon boss knew how the trouble would affect their businesses. The mayor was also worried and called a hasty meeting of the council to discuss matters.

They sat in his cramped office nursing their glasses of whiskey as they argued about what was happening in their normally peaceful town. There could be fights and shoot-outs when the ranch hands came in to spend their wages. Trouble on the range could hold back the possibilities of a railroad link. Even the telegraph line could be cut if matters got out of hand.

Mayor Raynor banged on his desk to gain some

attention. As the owner of the biggest dry-goods store, he felt the tension as much as anybody.

'Now, let's take this calmly,' he cautioned when they had all quietened down. 'Our main concern has gotta be this town. We need the ranchers and I can't argue that point. But this place comes first. Whoever wins a range war will have to come back here when it's all over. We got the goods and services they need. And it's the prosperity of Elverton that will bring in the railroad. So, let them fight among themselves without us takin' sides. Then, when it's finished, we'll be everybody's friend. How does that sound?'

There was a muttering around the office as they discussed the mayor's cynical but practical words.

'And if they're gonna fight,' the old judge mused in his usual gravelly voice, 'they'll sure as hell need supplies. You can't fight a war without guns and ammunition. Some of the store owners should do a good trade.'

He winked broadly at Hans Feldman and the gunsmith cheered up at the thought.

'But we stay neutral,' the mayor insisted.

They all nodded agreement and the meeting broke up on an optimistic note.

The council meeting was not the only gathering in the next few days. Local ranchers had arranged a meeting of their own at the home of Les Weldon.

94

His spread was the most central for travelling, and the cattlemen converged on his large ranch house four days after the council meeting.

Harry Vernon seemed reluctant to be part of it, but the others were eager and angry. They all knew of Lars Peterson's guns, and they had all lost cattle in the past few months. Their voices were raised as they tried to decide on what action to take. Peterson had no friends amongst them. His pious preaching and aloofness had only made him enemies in the thirty years he had lived in the area.

It was Art Rubin who appeared to speak for most of them. There were nods and grunts of agreement as he attempted to sum up their position.

'As I see it,' the thickset man said angrily, 'we are several thousand head of cattle down. Peterson's lost none. That don't make sense. Then we hear that fellas employed by him have raided the stage to try and get at the money Harry Vernon here was bringin' into town. Now we find he's havin' guns delivered. What could any rancher want with two dozen Winchester carbines? We ain't got no Indians raidin' us, and there are as sure as hell enough guns on any one of our ranches. I figure he aims to run us out and take over. So we gotta stop him.'

Vic Lawrence gave a loud cough in the slight

95

silence that followed Art Rubin's angry outburst. They all looked at the thin figure that sprawled in the cane chair. Vic Lawrence was a quiet man, and all respected his cool intelligence. He was a man who only spoke when he really had something to say. The rest of the time he spent chewing tobacco.

'Lars Peterson holds a prayer-meetin' every Sunday mornin' outside his ranch house,' he said in a thin voice. 'All his hands and the family are expected to be there. All in one place at the same time. And do folks carry guns at a prayer-meetin' on a Sunday?'

He looked around with a slight smile on his crooked lips. It took a moment for the meaning to sink in, but as it did, there were grins all round.

'Will our men fight?' Les Weldon asked uneasily after a while.

'They will if they wanta keep their jobs,' Art Rubin said.

Harry Vernon held up a restraining hand.

'I figure as how we should wait until my nephew gets back from the railhead,' he said thoughtfully. 'He might get a lead on the rustlin' that will give us somethin' more to go on.'

'Well, I reckon as how we have enough to go on,' Art Rubin snapped, 'and the longer we leave it, the tougher things will be.'

There was general agreement on that point and

Harry Vernon spread his hands in surrender. Sunday was to be the day of reckoning.

The four men who had lost cattle were men used to fighting for what they felt was their right. Each one told his hands about the situation and bought a little extra loyalty with promises of bonus pay when the job was done.

Lars Peterson was not popular with anybody. Neither were his hands. They seemed to drink less than other cowpokes and were mocked for carrying prayer-books wherever they went. Guns were cleaned and loaded, and each ranch headed for the Peterson spread to meet up by dawn on Sunday morning. It was a journey of two days or more for three of the ranches and even Harry Vernon would need a full day to get into position for an early morning attack. Chuck wagons had to accompany them and Wally drove his mules at a steady pace.

Harry Vernon rode hunched in his saddle while Wally was cheerful and seemed to be aching for a fight. Harry's little army of eleven men halted for the Saturday night at a small creek just four miles away from the Peterson ranch house. They were joined by twelve more men headed by Les Weldon. He was Harry's nearest neighbour and closest friend.

An advance rider from the other two groups

97

came to the creek to tell them that Vic Lawrence and Art Rubin were still a few miles behind but would join them just after dawn. Art was travelling with eight hands and Vic Lawrence had mustered twenty-one men. His group included his brother and three sons. The little army was a formidable force against the ten or twelve hands who would be gathered at the Peterson ranch house.

They were all gathered together just after sunrise on Sunday. Guns were checked and even the horses seemed to sense that something was in the air. They jerked their heads with excitement that was communicated to them by the actions of their nervous riders. The ranch owners reviewed their little army with a feeling of content.

At a signal from Art Rubin they set out on their last four miles. The morning was beginning to warm up and a slight breeze stirred the grass, blowing away the mists of the night. As they breasted a long, gentle rise, Vic Lawrence took out his watch and checked the time.

'I reckon as how they'll be in their go-to-meetin' mood by now,' he said.

There were a few grins as they looked down on the back of the adobe ranch house and the outbuildings that occupied three sides of a large square. Almost as though Vic Lawrence had said something prophetic, the sound of singing rose to their ears as Lars Peterson and his family led the worship in front of their home.

The rough and rather reluctant voices of the Peterson ranch hands joined in, and Harry Vernon thought that he could hear the sound of a harmonium in the background.

Art Rubin looked round at his men, then dug spurs into his mount. He shot forward at a gallop, a Colt .45 held high in his right hand as he led a wild charge down the slope and round the end of a row of store buildings and a bunkhouse.

Wally Payne looked on from the seat of his chuck wagon. Like any seasoned agitator, he could wave a sabre with the best but always stayed out of the line of fire. He cursed vividly at the way the wild charge had developed. If the self-satisfied leaders had listened to him their men would have fired with carbines from secure positions. They would have picked off the enemy without exposing themselves. He watched as the singing stopped and shouts filled the air. Shots were being fired. They were as wild as the charge and horsemen whooped and hollered in the centre of the large square in front of the Peterson home.

Harry Vernon rode reluctantly. He saw Ma Peterson and another woman ushering three young children into the building. The harmonium stood forlorn and the hymn-book, open above the keyboard, fluttered its pages like some distress signal.

Lars Peterson was there amongst his men. Tall and thin, and looking like some revival of Abraham Lincoln, he was shouting for calm and appeared to be pleading for the shooting to stop. He was gunned down to lie writhing on the gravelly earth. None of the hymn-singing hands appeared to be armed and the horsemen circled them with guns blazing until all were dead or wounded and a sudden lull fell over the scene.

The chuck wagons were arriving now. It was soon apparent why they were needed. Some of the attackers started to dismount and were heading for the house until Harry Vernon spurred his horse to place himself between them and the closed door.

'Just hold it there, fellas!' he shouted. 'There are women and children inside and they ain't got no part in any of this. Some of you go find a rig of some sort and hitch up a horse. Then they can pack a few things and leave. We don't make war on women and children.'

The other ranch owners nodded their agreement, and while the bunkhouse and the stores were being looted, a small four-wheeled wagonette was found and an elderly gelding was put in the shafts. It was Art Rubin who entered the house and was soon ushering Ma Peterson, her daughter-in-law and the three children to take their seats on it. They carried a few valuables, and after a weeping glance at the bodies around the yard, they drove off to the west.

There was an instant rush as the ranch hands began their plunder. The chuck wagons were soon loaded with everything movable, and even the curtains on the shining windows were pulled down. Nobody knew who started the fire, but as the last of the looters left the building it began to burn and the horsemen withdrew to a safer distance.

The four ranch owners sat their horses near a water-trough. The animals drank quietly and with complete indifference to what was happening around them.

'I guess we've put an end to the rustlin' in these parts.' Art Rubin grinned. 'And we've got one hell of a lotta cattle to divide up. That's a fair trade for what we've lost in the last few months, I reckon.'

Vic Lawrence nodded in agreement.

'And we got ourselves one hell of a stretch of grazin' as well,' he said thoughtfully. 'Willard's Creek and them timber areas belong to us now.'

As if the same realization had struck each man simultaneously, the four ranchers looked at each other with a sudden dawning mistrust.

TEN

Ryton was a small town. It existed only because the water supply was good and could cater for the herds of cattle that made the long trek to the new railhead on the outskirts. This single track, heading almost due north, joined the main east to west line at Pueblo.

Cattle-pens covered a huge acreage. Long fenced-in lanes led to the railroad line where ramps could load the animals for their final journey to the big cities in the East. It was the quiet time of the year now. The main part of the season was over and most of the pens were empty. A few mournful cattle were still waiting to be shipped, but it would be another three months before things got busy again.

Phil Jones was glad to see the little town. It had taken him the best part of seven days to reach it. The heat and flies had plagued him and his animals as they sweated over the rough trail. Phil reached Ryton in the late afternoon, camped on the outskirts away from the smell of the pens, and went into town early the next morning. His mule and cow pony found themselves hitched to a rail outside a meeting-house. It appeared to be the only deserted spot in town.

The marshal's office was easy to find. It was one of the few buildings not made of wooden planking. Its adobe walls were a startling white. Marshal Paton was a big man who sweated from every pore and kept wiping his face with a large bandanna.

'Sure we got stolen cattle through here.' He grinned. 'I figure as how there's more crooked dealings in my town than in any of them big places the writer fellas keep tellin' us about in the dime novels.'

'So you'd have some buyers who never asked questions?' Phil suggested quietly.

The marshal grinned again and fanned himself with a couple of sheets of paper.

'I reckon Leo Grange is your man. The other dealers ain't around much at this time of the year. But Leo's had deliveries of animals in the last few weeks. Different brands on them. A real mixed bunch. But that ain't proof of it bein' dishonest. There's often other brands mixed in with regular herds. The ranchers work things out among themselves.'

Phil nodded his understanding. 'How would Leo Grange handle the money side of things?' he asked.

'Well, if the deal was honest, most ranchers have the money paid into the local bank and then it's transferred, or they use them newfangled cheque things. Cash money in the hand is more likely if the cattle is rustled.'

He got up from the desk with evident difficulty and crossed to the stove to pour out some coffee for the two of them.

'You may be thinking, young fella,' he said as he handed over the mug, 'that I ain't runnin' things too well in this town. Well, I ain't. I keeps my job because I stays outa trouble. The folks what run this place is all in the cattle-dealin' business one way or another. They don't want things upset by nosy lawmen who go around arrestin' folk just because they bring a few stolen cattle to market. You savvy?'

'I savvy.'

'Good. So try not to involve me when you go around askin' questions.'

He gave a nod of dismissal. Phil finished his drink and headed for the door. The marshal had one last word to say.

'Leo Grange ain't the good-natured, go-to-meetin' sorta fella you'd like as a neighbour,' he said carefully. 'I hopes as how you're good with a gun. And watch out for his boy. He ain't wearin' no halo as I ever noticed.'

Phil Jones nodded his thanks and left the sweating lawman to nurse his coffee.

The young deputy walked down the lines of cattle-pens and glanced at the animals that occupied the few nearest to the rail track. He did not recognize any of the brands and soon learned from an old-timer that some steers had been shipped out a couple of days earlier.

He saw the little wood-built office of Leo Grange. It was just round the corner at the end of the main street, overlooking a line of pens and reached by a short flight of wooden steps. The door was open and he could catch a glimpse of a large man in shirt-sleeves. Phil hesitated for a moment. He had no powers in Ryton and could not rely on help from the marshal in an emergency. He decided to try a less obvious approach. He removed his badge and slipped it into the pocket of his shirt. Then he climbed the creaking steps and knocked on the open door.

Leo Grange was at a small table, looking at a sheaf of papers that bore the letter-heading of a rail company.

'What'll you be wantin' with me, fella?' he bawled at the intruder.

'You bein' a cattle-dealer, I thought as how you might be able to help,' Phil said meekly. He

105

stepped into the little room to confront the man. 'I've got a few head of steers just outside town and I'd sure be interested in sellin' them at a fair price.'

Leo Grange put down the papers and stared at the newcomer. His face was dark and fleshy, with eyes that seemed nearly closed under heavy brows.

'Ain't the season,' he growled, 'but there will be another freight train stoppin' here in six or seven days. We gotta feed them till then, so that's gotta be considered. How many steers you got?'

'Well, I ain't counted for the last few days, but I figure as about a hundred and fifty. We lost a few on the way.'

'That ain't many. On the way from where?'

Phil tried to look a little shifty.

'Well, we bought steers in several places. From homesteaders mostly. We came by them honestly, if that's what's worryin' you.'

The dealer almost managed a smile.

'It ain't worryin' me,' he said, 'but I take it that they all have different brands?'

'Sort of.'

'Bring 'em into town then and I'll sort out a pen for you. I suppose you want payin' in cash money?'

The words were said almost with a sneer.

'Yeah, cash money. We ain't got no bank.'

'Fair enough. Bring them in before dark and maybe we can settle things tonight.'

The two men parted, Phil tramping down the wooden steps and Leo Grange watching him from the doorway of the office. When the young deputy was almost out of sight, the dealer ran down the steps and round the corner where a group of men were talking. He grabbed one of them by the arm.

'Go follow that fella at the far end of the east pens. I want to know everythin' he does. He says he's got cattle to trade, but he don't smell like a fella what's been herdin' steers for any length of time. Find out how many men are with him and where they're makin' camp.'

The young man nodded without saying a word. He hitched up the gun at his waist and hurried after Phil Jones. The cattle-dealer went back to his office to sit thoughtfully behind the table.

Phil turned on to the main street and walked slowly back to where he had left his animals. He was experienced enough to know that he was being followed. The marshal had mentioned that Leo Grange had a boy. The deputy guessed that the young fellow who was just turning the corner of the side lane could be the one. He was reflected in the window of a hardware store, and Phil deliberately looked at the goods on display so that he could get a better view of his follower.

The young fellow was tall and slim, with fair hair and a thin face. He kept one hand on the gun at his side and looked as if he could use it. The street was getting busy now as the stores began to open while children crawled to school. Phil reached the meeting-house where his animals greeted him with total indifference. He noticed that the door of the building was open and decided to add extra mystery to his activities in town.

It was cold inside the meeting-house and the place smelled of lamp-oil and burnt tallow. An elderly preacher in dark clothes was sitting at an organ. He was arranging the music and playing a few notes as he decided what to use. He took his hands off the keys and his feet off the pedals when he saw a visitor. His lined face broke into a smile of welcome.

'We are not really having a meeting today,' he explained apologetically. 'This is all in preparation for a funeral this afternoon. Are you by any chance one of the MacDonald family?'

'No, Reverend,' Phil said as he displayed his badge. 'I'm checkin' on some cattle rustlers. They may have come this way to sell to the dealers at the railhead. I was really expectin' to meet one of our local ranchers here. Mr Peterson. He's out makin' a few enquiries himself. Said he was comin' to Ryton and we could get together.'

'Ah, Mr Peterson.' The reverend preacher nodded his head. 'Ah, yes, I know him. He always looks in on us when he comes to town with cattle. Brings his hands with him too. A very worthy man,

Deputy. A very worthy man. But I haven't seen him since the last drive. That's nearly six months ago.'

The old man paused for a moment as though some thought had crossed his mind.

'It's a strange thing,' he said slowly, 'but I heard that he was in town only a couple of weeks or so ago. He seems to have kept out of sight and somebody said that he visited the saloon. That doesn't sound like Lars Peterson. He's always taken a strong stand against the demon drink.'

He shook his head sadly while Phil crossed to the window to pull aside the heavy drapes and look out. His young shadow was standing across the street, nearly hidden by the vertical wooden sign of a livery stable.

'Perhaps it was somebody else, Reverend,' he suggested softly.

'I do hope so. I do indeed hope so.'

Phil thanked the preacher for his help and took a quick glance round the room. There was a rear door, as he had felt there must be in the long, narrow structure. He moved swiftly between the rows of benches and let himself out into a smelly back lane. It took only a short run between the wooden buildings until he could get across the main street and behind the livery stable. He moved quietly until he could see the back of the young fellow who was still watching from behind the wooden signboard.

Phil drew his gun and poked it firmly into the man's back.

'One wrong move, fella,' he whispered gently, 'and I'll blow a hole clean through you.'

The young man reached automatically for the gun at his side, but Phil knocked his hand away and took the .44 Remington from the holster. He stuck it into his own belt.

'Let's take a short walk,' he suggested with another sharp prod from his own gun.

He guided his prisoner down the side lane and along past some empty cattle-pens. There was a small hut on the corner of another lane. The door was ajar and Phil glanced in. The place was empty of everything except a few bales of straw and a rat that scuttled away as the shadows moved and the door creaked.

'In here,' the deputy said as he pushed his prisoner ahead of him.

He closed the door once they were inside and leaned against it. The man stood facing him now, about six feet away, his face a mask of hatred and fear.

'We don't like bein' held up in this town,' he snarled in an attempt at bravado. 'We got laws.'

'I am the law, fella.' Phil grinned in the gloom. 'And I'm holdin' a gun. And any knowin' lawyer will have to admit that a gun is mighty good law. Now suppose you tell me what orders Leo Grange

110

gave you.'

'I don't know what the hell you're talkin' about.'

'In that case you're of no use to me and I might as well kill you now. I'll just go back and ask Leo the questions.'

He raised the gun and the young fellow spread his hands wildly.

'All right! Don't get all het up, fella. He just told me to follow you and tell him what you was doin' in town.'

'Are you his son?'

'Hell, no. I just work for him. And he's one tough *hombre*.'

'Ever heard tell of Lars Peterson?'

There was a long silence that was only broken when Phil Jones raised the gun a little.

'Sure. He was in town last week. Or maybe the week before. Came in with three or four of his men and sold Leo some cattle. They was shipped out a few days back.'

'All with different brands?'

The youth managed a grin.

'Sure.'

'What do you know about Peterson?' Phil asked.

The man shrugged. 'Ain't hardly seen him. He's one big fella in the ranchin' business, so I'm told.'

'But you see him every time he comes into town?'

111

'No, not till this last visit. Fellas like Peterson don't mix with fellas like me. But I did see him in the saloon with a couple of his hands. One of them is still in town.'

Phil blinked. 'Is he now? And where would I find him?'

The man shrugged. 'In the saloon, I guess. He seems to have money to spend. Look, fella, what's all this about? I'm just doin' my job, and I ain't lookin' for no trouble.'

'Then go work for somebody else. Leo Grange will be warmin' a seat in the county jail before long. And a few of his friends will be keepin' him company. Don't be one of them.'

'Are you really a lawman?'

Phil pulled the badge out of his pocket and held it so that the engraved lettering could not be read.

'Federal marshal,' he said. 'We're cleanin' up the cattle business in Ryton. Take a hint, fella, leave town.'

'You're lettin' me go?'

'I ain't got no reason to hold you,' Phil assured him, 'unless you go keepin' company with Leo Grange. Just get on your horse and get the hell out.'

The young man turned to leave and then stopped in the doorway.

'My gun?' he suggested almost shyly.

'Buy another one.'

There was no argument and Phil watched the man hurry down the lane. He waited until he was out of sight and then walked slowly back to Leo Grange's office. The big man was still at the table, drinking coffee and with a newpaper in front of him. He seemed surprised and a little nervous at the appearance of Phil Jones. He looked past him through the open doorway in the apparent hope that his assistant might be in attendance.

'What would you be wantin' this time?' he asked gruffly.

'Just a passin' call to tell you that the fella you sent after me is on his way outa town. You're on your own now, fella.'

The cattle-dealer half-rose from his chair. Then he decided against it as Phil towered over him.

'So he left town,' he managed to say. 'So what?'

'Why is one of Lars Peterson's men still in Ryton?'

The words took the man by surprise.

'How the hell would I know?' he asked angrily. 'He just stayed on after we'd done the deal, I suppose. Look, fella, I only buy and sell cattle. I don't go around askin' questions. Are you the law or something?'

'Federal law. That's why your hired help has quit. So where do I find this fella from the Peterson spread?'

113

The cattle-dealer spread his hands in what was clearly a gesture of defeat.

'He's at Ma Burton's boardin' house. It's just back of the main street, right behind the pharmacy. He drinks at the White Horse most nights.'

Phil nodded his thanks and left the office. He was hoping that the young fellow had really left town and looked up and down the lane and along the main street anxiously.

Ma Burton's place was not hard to find. It was the usual clapboard house with a sheltering porch. The windows shone cleanly and there were curtains in bright colours. A few horses stood at the hitching-rail. Phil was undecided for a moment. He needed to ask questions, but there were so many things he did not know, and some of the stories he had already been told did not make a lot of sense.

As he stood there he spotted a man coming along the street. It was the bandaged head and stiff right arm that drew his attention. He had seen the fellow before. When he was a prisoner in Elverton jailhouse.

ELEVEN

Phil's breath came in a sharp hiss as he reached down for the gun at his waist. His opponent was not quite within range. He had stopped in his tracks as he recognized the deputy marshal. The man hesitated for a moment and then went for his own Colt. He was using the left hand and was slower in his movements.

Phil opened fire, The bullet tore through the man's right arm just above the elbow. He staggered back a step or so as he fired at Phil. His bullet went wide and the deputy was able to take aim again. It was the tethered horses at the rail of the boarding-house that spoiled his chance of a good shot. One of them shied at the noise and broke loose. It dashed between the two men and almost bumped into Phil Jones.

He found himself dodging the flying hoofs and then felt a dig in the back as one of the other animals swung round so that its rump caught him. He nearly dropped the Colt, and by the time his hand was steady again the man had run across the street and into an alley. Phil cursed audibly and dashed after him. He could see the marshal emerging from the jailhouse while people were sheltering in doorways but staring out so that they would miss nothing of interest.

When Phil reached the alley there was no sign of his opponent. It was a long, shadowy place with rubbish piling up, and only the side doors of two stores to break the lines of weathered boards. He advanced slowly, hearing the footsteps of the marshal gaining on him. The big lawman caught up and eyed him suspiciously.

'I don't want no gunplay in Ryton,' he warned. 'Who the hell was you shootin' at back there?'

Phil told him and the marshal seemed appeased a little. They came to the end of the little passage-way and stood uncertainly as they viewed the lines of empty cattle-pens, small sheds and privies that covered the area. There was nobody in sight and a solitary mule stared at them as it chewed on some fodder.

'I reckon as how he's in one of them sheds,' the marshal said nervously. 'I ain't figurin' on tryin' all them doors without some back-up.'

Phil was looking at the ground and eventually spotted some fresh blood that made an uncertain trail off to their left. He pointed to it silently and led the way along the wide and rutted path looking for more signs to follow. They passed one small store hut and came to a halt in front of another where two bloodstains were clear in the sand by the closed door. People were beginning to come on the scene now. They kept well away at the end of the little alleys, but did not want to miss anything exciting. Phil caught a glimpse of Leo Grange on the steps of his office. He had a carbine under his arm.

The marshal put a hand on the rope that held the large wooden door-bolt. He seemed about to pull it but then changed his mind.

'He could be lyin' for us,' he said bleakly. 'We need to get a few of the folks to back us up.'

Phil looked round. It did not appear to him that the locals were likely to volunteer. He spotted a wooden bucket a few yards away and went to collect it. The lawman watched him nervously.

'Open the door when I give you the nod,' Phil told him. 'I'll sling this in and that'll sure as hell start him shootin' if he's there. Then we can rush him while he's still wonderin' what in hell's happened.'

The marshal did not seem very happy to do any rushing but he was prepared to open the door and stand behind it while the younger man took all the risks. Phil gave the marshal a nod when he was

117

ready. The frail wooden panels groaned as the latch was pulled back and the door swung open. The interior of the dark shed was suddenly illuminated by a shaft of brilliant sunlight.

Phil flung in the pail and then drew his gun to await a reaction. Nothing happened.

There was a long moment of silence and then a shout split the air. One of the onlookers pointed to a figure standing on the wooden steps of Leo Grange's office. The cattle-dealer had raised the carbine to his shoulder and was pointing it towards the marshal and Phil Jones.

The big lawman ducked for cover round the side of the shed while Phil raised his gun to take a chance shot at a range that he knew was too great. The cattle-dealer opened fire and there was a yell of pain from somewhere behind the little shed. Then the cattle-dealer put down his gun and pointed with a grin to his victim. The bandaged hold-up man staggered from behind the shed. Blood flowed from high in his chest. He clutched his body as he blundered unseeing into the hands of the lawmen.

Things happened quickly after that. The wounded man was carried to the jailhouse and the doctor sent for. Leo Grange joined the two lawmen and was quick to point out how law-abiding he was. He had noticed the man tear away a few of the planks at the back of the shed. He had seem him emerge and get ready to crawl off into the maze of cattle-pens.

The marshal was quick to pour a drink for the cattle-dealer and they were soon joined by the mayor. It was half an hour before the doctor emerged from the cell where his patient lay on the bunk with his chest heavily bound. There was also a fresh bandage round his right arm which the doctor had placed in a splint. He took a drink from the marshal and sat down wearily in front of the desk.

'He ain't gonna last long,' he said as he sipped the cheap liquid. 'There's been too much blood lost and I ain't bettin' on him makin' the night. Just let him sleep, and if he wants a drink or anything, let him have it. It won't do no harm now.'

The little group split up eventually and only the marshal and Phil remained in the jailhouse with the dying man. Phil volunteered to stay there for the night so that the marshal could get off home and sleep with his equally large wife. The local lawman was delighted at the offer and hurried off soon after. Phil crossed to the cell and looked through the bars. The prisoner was still sedated and was snoring loudly. Some blood had stained the outer bandage on his arm where Phil had shot him. The wrapping round the chest was still pristine white.

It was an hour later while Phil was dozing in the large leather chair, that the man woke with a muttered groan. Phil got up and crossed the office to look at him.

'You want somethin' to drink?' he asked.

The prisoner looked at him with slightly dazed eyes.

'No, I guess not,' he muttered. 'I ain't gonna get away from this one, am I?'

'Well, you might pull through. These things happen.'

'No, I heard what the doc said. I was just goin' off at the time, but he has a loud voice. I ain't gonna live to be hanged. I figure as how I owe all this trouble to my friends. They sure been shootin' the hell outa me, one way and another.'

He almost managed a chuckle as he spoke. He licked his dry lips and Phil crossed to the water-jug and tipped a drop into a tin mug. He entered the cell and placed it to the parched lips.

'Thanks,' the man said softly. 'Do you reckon as how revenge is a good thing, Marshal?'

'Yeah, I do, when you can't get justice. It's sometimes the only thing a man has left.'

'That's how I figure it right now. I've got one hell of a story to tell you and I don't want to die while the bastards who got me into this are walkin' free.'

'Well, I'm here to listen.'

'Well, me and four other fellas makes ourselves a decent livin' by robbin' stages and freight wagons. Folk don't usually get hurt and there are fellas in various towns what tell us when a stage is carryin' somethin' worth having. My contact in Elverton sent a message that the stage would be carryin' seven thousand dollars in cash money. Well, you know what happened. We held it up and got nothin' worth the trouble.'

He gestured for another drop of water and Phil helped him get the mug to his lips.

'So I decided to ride into Elverton and meet up with my contact. Somethin' had gone wrong, and I didn't reckon it to be his fault. I figured that they'd be puttin' the cash on another stage or maybe sendin' it through on one of the freight wagons. He might have the latest news, or could maybe give us another lead.'

The man sat up a little but fell back with a groan.

'It sure hurts,' he murmured as he tried to get himself into a more comfortable position. 'Anyways, I hadn't reckoned on that damned woman stayin' overnight at Elverton. She spotted me and you know what happened then. I was in one hell of a mess.'

'Who killed Marshal Anderson?' Phil's voice was harsh as he waited for the answer he felt was now a certainty.

'Don't be in such a hurry, fella,' the man whispered with an attempt at a grin. 'I'm not leavin' anythin' out. The fella in Elverton who was tellin' me tales outa school was real worried. I guess he felt that I might talk if the marshal started beattn' the hell outa me. Maybe I would have. You can never tell. So he came to the window of my cell and let fly with a scatter-gun. I was sure lucky not to get it full in the face.'

'Who was it, fella? Who was it?'

The man told him and Phil sucked in his breath at the name.

'Go on,' he said, 'you're sure gonna have a nice revenge when I get back to town.'

'If you don't get yourself killed along the line. Just play things safe, Marshal. Until you get back home and blow all these high-falutin folk apart.'

Phil grinned. 'I'll do just that,' he assured the man. 'So what happened next?'

'Well, the night that all the trouble started in town, I was pretty edgy. The marshal just sat there, glarin' at me, and you were out tryin' to cool things down. Then there was a loud knock at the back door of the jailhouse. It sure made me jump. I thought a lynch mob had come a-callin' on me. The marshal goes down the passage and I hear him askin' who's there. Then he opens the back door and this fella comes in. Real friendly they was and the marshal goes to the desk. I reckon he was gonna take out the whiskey-bottle.'

The prisoner shook his head almost sadly and winced in pain as he did so.

'Then this fella pulls a gun and clobbers the marshal. I could hear his skull crack from where I was. The next thing, I'm bein' let outa the cells and rushed to the back door. My new boss is waitin' there with two other fellas. The one who did the clobberin' rides off and we're all outa Elverton as smooth as fresh shortenin' bread.'

He lay back, exhausted from speaking while Phil waited impatiently for him to get some energy back again. It was a long wait and the young deputy began to worry in case the prisoner died without saying anything else. Then there was a sharp cough and the man opened his eyes again.

'I seem to have no breath,' he gasped. 'What was I sayin' just now? Yeah, I recall. Well, this new boss man didn't help me outa the goodness of his heart. He had a deal to make. If I told him who tipped me off about the money on the stage, he'd give me a steady job at good pay.'

'And you told him?'

'Fella, I was gonna be hanged, one way or another. And this old coot had saved my skin. I reckoned he weren't no go-to-meetin' preacher fella, so we could do business. Sure I told him, and he brought me here to Ryton with some cattle to sell. Leo Grange bought them and that's why he just tried to kill me. He knew he was buyin' stolen steers and he knew the name of my new boss. I reckon Leo didn't want me tellin' you no tales. He must be one worried man right now.'

'He must be,' Phil agreed impatiently. 'But tell me, who is this new boss you signed up with?'

The man had to struggle to get his breath.

'A fella by the name of Lars Peterson,' he wheezed.

TWELVE

Phil rode slowly back to Elverton. The last words of the hold-up man were still eating into his thoughts. They were unsettling and he was trying to figure out how to break the news to the mayor and his new boss, Marshal Ed Welsey.

The town was strangely quiet when he arrived. People just looked at him almost as though he were a stranger. Faces were shuttered and heads turned away. He tethered his two animals outside the jailhouse and went in to report to Marshal Welsey. The new lawman was sitting at his desk writing very slowly in the large book that carried the weekly report for the mayoral office.

'Well, did you track down the rustlin' fellas?' Phil was asked as the man thankfully put down his pen. 'You sure been gone long enough.'

'It's quite a journey to the railhead and back

again,' Phil said slowly.

He crossed to the stove and took off the coffee-pot. The enamelled mugs all looked dirty, so he changed his mind and sat down opposite his boss.

'What's the matter with this town?' he asked. 'Folks were all lookin' at me real strange-like. I felt as welcome as a temperance preacher.'

Marshal Welsey hesitated for a moment. He was a big man in his thirties. A wide, open face gave him a stupid look and anybody who knew him well would go along with that assessment. He rose from the chair and reached out for his hat.

'Things have been happenin' here,' he said shortly. 'I think we'd better go see the mayor. He'll want to know all about the chase he sent you on.'

Without more ado he led the way from the office and down the street to the mayor's store. They were told that the First Citizen was across at the bank and would be back in half an hour or so. The men took seats on a couple of empty wooden crates that had once held tins of coffee. They waited impatiently until the stout figure of Bert Raynor appeared through the door. He was wiping his brow and looked rather flustered. His mood did not seem to be lifted by the reappearance of Phil Jones. He merely led the way to his office and waved them both to chairs.

'So, how did you get on?' he asked bleakly.

'I tracked down some rustled cattle and the man they was sold to,' Phil said carefully. 'I also caught up with the fella what escaped from the jailhouse. He's dead.'

The mayor's face brightened a little and he straightened up in his seat.

'Is that a fact now?' he exclaimed. 'Well, you ain't wasted your time, young fella. And did you find out who was behind the rustlin' business?'

'Yes. Lars Peterson.'

The mayoral face broke into a smile. 'Well, ain't that just dandy!' he crowed. 'That news will bring back a few smiles around this miserable town. You've sure as hell brought Elverton welcome tidings this day, Phil. You've done a good job.'

The young man looked from one to the other of his two colleagues in puzzlement.

'Why?' he murmured. 'What's been happenin' while I've been away?'

'You ain't told him?' The mayor looked at the marshal.

Ed Welsey shook his head. 'No, Uncle Bert. I brought him straight across to you.'

'Yeah, sure. You did the right thing, son. Well, young Phil, your uncle and the other ranchers made a raid on Peterson's place. They killed him and his sons. His wife and the rest of the family have departed for parts unknown. It was one hell of a slaughter. Folks in town ain't happy about it. And you're one of the Vernons, so I guess they look at you a bit peculiar. But this news makes all the difference. We'll tell folks all about the affair, and things will get back to normal in no time.'

Phil was silent for a moment. This was not the sort of homecoming he had expected.

'So what happens to Lars Peterson's stock and land?' he asked slowly.

The mayor shrugged. 'Well, that's what's been rilin' folks. The ranchers have divided everythin' up between them. But now that we know Peterson was tryin' to harm his neighbours, it's all for the best. What else did you find out?'

He leaned forward eagerly in the hope of more good news.

'The hold-up man talked before he died,' Phil told him. 'He felt that some folks had done him dirty, and he reckoned to get even. He told me who gave him the information about the stage carryin' my uncle's money.'

'Who?'

Phil knew that he had the avid attention of the other two men.

'That bankin' fella, Will Halliday,' he said.

The mayor's mouth fell open and he stared straight ahead for a moment. Then his face broke into a radiant smile as he rose from his chair and broke out the best whiskey.

'Well, if that don't beat the big bass drum!' he crowed. 'That money-lendin' bastard has been makin' a few extra dollars by helpin' stage hold-up fellas. You have made me a very happy man, young Phil. I reckon as how a rise in pay is on the cards right now.'

'You want me to go and arrest him, Uncle Bert?' Ed Welsey asked eagerly.

'Hell, no. I'll just go along and tell our Shylock that he takes orders from us from now onwards. Let me tell you fellas that we now run the bank in this town. And don't it feel real good? I just spent the worst half-hour of my life with that poisonous toad. I needed to raise a loan to get some new stock for the comin' season. He wants I should use my home and the store as collateral. Me! The mayor of this place, being put in that position. I wanted to spit in his eye. Well, now I can. Now I can go back there and do a deal that won't cost me one bent cent in interest. He's gonna crawl from now on.'

He looked at the two men, his face shining with sweat and his eyes bright.

'Now this is just between the three of us. Just remember that,' he cautioned. 'This town is now on the mend and business will start boomin' again when all the ranchers settle down and the cattle season starts up. I can see us havin' the railroad here faster than we coulda hoped. With the bank in our pockets, we can sure look to a prosperous future.'

Phil decided to say no more. He left the office soon after and went to unsaddle his cow pony and the patient mule. He had a meal at the boarding-house where he lodged, and then dozed until the evening.

The saloon was crowded that night and word had already gone around town about the guilt of Lars Peterson. People were now friendlier and Phil received a few welcomes as he went to the bar for a glass of beer. He was on the look-out for somebody and he soon spotted the man he wanted to see. Banker Halliday was holding court amid a little crowd of sycophantic courtiers, all of whom owed him money. He caught Phil's eye and raised his glass in a condescending salute. It did not seem that the mayor had yet spoiled his evening by mentioning the latest news. Phil waited patiently.

It was another half-hour before the First Citizen turned up and joined the banker. He soon drew the man away from the crowd and Phil could see the change of expression on Will Halliday's face as the two men talked. There was no doubt that the mayor was laying down the new rules for banking in the little town of Elverton. The money-lender had turned pale and there were beads of sweat on his forehead that shone in the lamplight. He left the saloon soon afterwards and the mayor happily joined his friends and cheerfully bought them all drinks.

Phil also left. He followed the banker down the busy main street and caught up with him on the corner by his own house.

'I'd like a few words with you, Mr Halliday,' the deputy said quietly.

'And I can guess what you're on about, young fella,' the banker snarled. 'Come and see me in my office tomorrow and you'll get your loan, the same as that damned mayor and his bone-headed nephew. But now just leave me in peace. My wife is waiting for me so I'll wish you a good night.'

'Don't be in such a hurry, Mr Halliday,' Phil said patiently. 'I only want a word. There's somebody else who will soon know about your contact with the stage-robbers. And he'll be wantin' a hell of a lot more than a bank loan.'

The money-lender stopped in his tracks. His doughy white hand was on the gate as he looked anxiously at the lawman.

'What the hell are you talkin' about, young fella?' he stammered. 'The mayor assured me that only you and that young pantywaist nephew of his knew about this affair. I made an error of judgement in a weak moment and now I must pay for it. So let's just leave it at that.'

'Before he died,' Phil said solemnly, 'that stage-robber wanted revenge on all the folks what let him down. He was real riled at them. And you'd tried to kill him with that scatter-gun. You was sure top of his list. So he sent a message to my Uncle Harry and the other ranchers. You've just seen what they do to folks who betray them. Lars Peterson and his sons are all dead. I can just imagine my uncle comin' whoopin' and hollerin' into town with all his hands. You'll probably be lynched outside your own bank and nobody will be interested in stoppin' them. Money-lenders ain't popular folk.'

The banker seemed about to faint. He grasped the gate hard and leaned against it. Phil smiled in the darkness.

'I could make a suggestion,' he said in a soothing voice. 'I'm not one of them fellas as needs a loan from your bank. You should know right well that money is not a problem with me. So I suggest you pack your goods and leave town quiet-like. Do it tonight and don't tell anybody where you're heading. And don't take any of the bank's money with you. I'd hate to be sent chasin' around tryin' to find you and bring you back for trial. After a talk like this, I wouldn't be wantin' to bring you back alive.'

The banker nodded silently and began to walk slowly up the path.

'There's just one more thing,' Phil called after

him. 'My uncle didn't want anyone to know about that money comin' into town. He sure didn't tell you about it. So who did?'

The banker stopped and half-turned.

'It was the fella he was buyin' the cattle from,' he said in a despairing voice. 'He owed money to the bank and I'd been pressin' him to clear his debt. Or at least reduce it. So he told me that he was getting cash from Harry Vernon for some cattle. It was coming in on the next stage.'

Phil nodded. It was more or less what he might have expected and he now knew what his next move must be.

'Just one more question,' he said almost fearfully.

The banker gave him the answer that he dreaded and Phil Jones walked thoughtfully away.

Phil Jones was on the main street early the next morning. He passed the closed bank and stopped outside the jailhouse. Ed Welsey was still abed and the young deputy moved on to the mayor's hardware store. One of the daughters was sweeping the stoop and informed him that her father was within and checking some goods in the back storeroom. Phil went through and found the mayor in his shirt-sleeves being helped by his other daughter. They were moving some barrels ready to be loaded on to a customer's rig.

The young deputy was greeted with a wide smile by Bert Raynor. Phil was now a mayoral favourite and he was ushered into the office with a friendly hand on his elbow.

'And what brings you here so early in the day, Phil?' the First Citizen asked as he settled back in his chair.

'I've been doin' a lotta thinkin' about that hold-up fella, Mr Mayor,' the deputy said slowly. 'He was real talkative about Lars Peterson. Even described him to me in a lotta detail. Even talked about the horse he was riding.'

He paused and shook his head as though bewildered.

'But it don't make a lotta sense,' he said. 'It just don't make no sense at all.'

'You'd better explain, son,' the mayor prompted as he felt in the desk drawer for a stogie. 'What don't make sense?'

Phil leaned forward and rested his hands on the desk.

'He said that he had a drink with Lars Peterson in the Ryton saloon. But Peterson never drank. He was a real abstainer. You know that as well as I do, Mayor.'

'Well, most of them fellas is hypocrites, son. What he wouldn't do round here, he might do some place where he wasn't known. Is that all?'

'No. He described Peterson. Red nose,

bearded, unwashed, and bow-legged. A man of about sixty-five to seventy. And carryin' a gun. That sure don't sound like Lars Peterson. The fella was also short and thickset. And rode a horse with the Vernon brand on it.'

The mayor put the cigar down with a slightly trembling hand. He sat thoughtfully for a moment.

'Wally Payne,' he muttered as if to himself. 'He was all for makin' trouble at the Peterson spread. Agitatin' all the time, the old devil was. Are you tellin' me that he's been behind all this trouble?'

'Could be.'

The mayor got up from his chair and began pacing the little office. He rubbed the side of his face with a restless hand and then stared out of the window with his breath steaming up the glass.

'How do you read this?' he asked Phil without turning round.

'Word is that Wally is kin to Uncle Harry and me,' Phil said as he swivelled round in his chair to look at the man. 'He's one hard fella and a big influence on Uncle Harry. It looks as if everythin' was started to try and make Peterson look like some rustlin' type who was out to harm the other ranchers. Those guns came into town addressed to him, but he never collected them even though he'd sent Ross Logan into town to pick up supplies. Anybody could have ordered them in his name. The rustlin' was done to concentrate thoughts on Peterson because his spread was never raided. Then this robber is freed from the jailhouse so that he can be taken to Ryton and left as bait for some rube like me. He's told that Peterson is his new boss, but Wally seems to have just left him there so that I'd pick him up. If Leo Grange had been a better shot, the whole thing would have worked.'

The mayor came back to the desk. He looked despondent now and the cigar had gone out.

'So what do we do?' he asked in a defeated voice.

'I want to keep out of it. Uncle Harry will probably stand by Wally and they're both my kin. You understand, Mr Mayor?'

'I do, son. I do. I'll send Ed out to the Vernon spread with a posse. He can bring Wally Payne back here and we'll ask the old devil a few questions.'

'They certainly need asking, Mr Mayor, but it might be easier to wait till Saturday,' Phil said with a slight wink. 'Wally likes to come into Elverton for a drink and stay at the edge of town camped in the chuck wagon overnight. It ain't pay week so he could well be the only one from the Vernon spread comin' to town. It would be better to pick him up after he'd had a few drinks and was bedded down. It'd be better than sendin' fellas out to the Vernon spread and riskin' a gunfight. It'd also save posse money.'

The mayor brightened up a little. 'That's a good idea, lad. It might also save a few lives.'

THIRTEEN

Elverton was a very disturbed town by the time Saturday arrived. The bank was closed. The manager had vanished with his wife and everything portable from their home. The keys had been left on the table and the marshal had to break in to find out what had happened. There was no message. Just a missing family along with their rig and the bay gelding that pulled it.

The chief clerk had checked the accounts but no money was missing. That at least allowed everybody to breathe freely again. The mayor was furious but there was nothing he could say or do. The bank would open again as normal on Monday morning, but the rumours would last for weeks. Coming on top of Lars Peterson's death and the huge changes in ranch ownership, folk were gossiping on every corner.

Wally Payne arrived as usual just after dusk. He drove the old chuck wagon and camped on the outskirts of town. Nobody at the Vernon ranch minded their cook going into Elverton for his weekly drink. A young lad took over his chores and did a much better job.

The old cook was at his accustomed place at the long counter of the Golden Bell when Marshal Welsey made his entrance. The lawman spotted him talking to a couple of younger men and hesitated for a moment before doing his job. It was the mayor who had decided on an arrest in the saloon. He was afraid that Wally might not stay camped in Elverton overnight, and he had doubts about Ed Welsey's ability to track the man in the darkness. He could also see the publicity being good for his own image of keeping law and order in the town.

It was all new to the marshal and he was not quite sure how to go about it. He had hoped that his deputy might be doing the job. The mayor had to explain in simple terms that being a lawman was more than wearing a badge and getting free drinks. Ed Welsey approached the bar and folks began to nudge each other at his presence. There was a sudden hush in their conversations.

'Wally,' the lawman said in a slightly hesitant voice, 'I gotta take you along to the jailhouse to answer a few questions. Just don't make no fuss and come along, quiet-like.'

Wally Payne held the whiskey glass half-way to his mouth as he stared at the man opposite. His short-sighted eyes held an impish humour as though he could not believe what he was hearing.

'You figurin' on arrestin' me, young fella?' he crowed as he looked round the saloon for the support of the other drinkers. 'You sure got big ideas since your uncle stuck that badge on you. Now be a good little lad and go play pinnin' the tail on the donkey along of all the other kids.'

The marshal flushed and his hand went down for the Colt at his waist.

'Wally, I ain't foolin' about!' he shouted angrily. 'You got one hell of a lotta questions to answer and I'm takin' you to the jailhouse. So move it, old fella.'

The elderly cook put down the glass and stood back from the bar counter.

'I may be an old man, Ed,' he said tersely, 'but I ain't yet met a fella who can take me.'

He drew his gun and pulled back the hammer. Ed Welsey did the same but was slightly quicker. Wally pressed the trigger with a sharp whoop of drunken delight. The bullet hit the marshal somewhere high in his left shoulder. He staggered back and fired with a sureness he never knew he possessed. The bullet took Wally Payne in the chest and the old man let out a little gasp before sliding gently to the sawdusted floor. There was a silence in the saloon as the smoke spiralled up to the brass oil-lamps.

The two young men who had been talking to Wally were the first to move. They knelt down as the old man breathed his last. Then they stood up slowly and faced the marshal. Both were armed and with the dust of travel on their clothes.

'You can't go round shootin' our kin,' one of them said bleakly. 'Killin' an old man what can hardly see ain't no brave thing to do, fella. You gotta pay for that.'

'He drew on me,' Ed Welsey protested. 'I was tryin' to arrest him. On the mayor's orders.'

He was desperately trying to recall the identity of the two men and began to realize that they were Harry Vernon's sons.

'This is law business,' he said with an attempt at authority. 'Don't get yourselves mixed up in it.'

'We are mixed up in it,' the other young man said. 'We can't go back to our pa and tell him that we stood by while some gun-happy small-town lawman killed our kin. You're gonna have to use that gun again, fella.'

The marshal looked from one to the other. He glanced wildly round the saloon, but there was no help written on any of the faces that stared at him from a safe distance. He looked again at his two opponents. They had reputations for being dim-witted and trigger-happy. It was a moment of decision and he had enough pride to know that he could not back down. The marshal put his thumb on the hammer of the Colt and watched as two eager hands reached down for the guns that would end his life.

'I wouldn't make any silly moves, fellas!'

The voice was loud and came from the other end of the bar. Everybody turned to look at the speaker. Phil Jones stood with a shotgun in his grasp. Both barrels were cocked and the weapon pointed at his two cousins. They moved their hands away from the holsters and stared at him in silence.

The young deputy came slowly across the floor. People moved away so that there was a large space around the little group. A scatter-gun was too dangerous a weapon with its wide spread of shot. Some of the spectators even decided to slip out of the door. Phil stopped within a few feet of the Vernon lads.

'Take their guns, Marshal,' he said quietly. 'and then we'll find them a nice cell for the night.'

One of the brothers found his voice and spit his anger at this family betrayal.

'Pa won't take this kindly, Phil,' he snarled. 'He'll be down on this town with all the hands he can muster. He'll break us outa that jailhouse faster than spit. And he'll be wantin' revenge for Uncle Wally.'

'I'll go tell your pa what happened,' Phil said. 'Wally has been sellin' stolen cattle and consortin' with folk what hold up stages. I got a lot to tell your pa.'

Excited talk broke out as soon as the marshal's little party left the saloon. Two hefty men carried away the body of Wally Payne and word spread round the town about the exciting happenings in the Golden Bell. Marshal Welsey was rather proud of himself. He sat at his desk while the doctor tended to the flesh wound that would make him a hero with a reputation as a tough lawman. His two prisoners sat miserably in a cell and Phil looked at them through the bars.

'Wally couldn't have done what he did without help,' he told them bluntly. 'He had to spend time away from the ranch. He had to have some of the hands ridin' alongside him. And he had to have a reason for all he did. So where do you fellas fit in?'

The younger Vernon lad came up to the bars and peered at Phil owlishly. Hal was the brighter of the two and some folk even said that he could read and write as well as a twelve-year-old.

'Pa was worried about Wally,' he said quietly. 'He'd go missin' for days on end and then claim he'd had a drinkin' bout. He never did much about the place anyways, so he was hardly missed. Pa sent us here tonight to keep an eye on him. There are three, maybe four fellas back on the spread who was rather friendly with him. They went missin' now and then as well. But it's hard to check when a fella says he's been roundin' up strays. We didn't think of them doin' the rustlin' though. It's sure been worryin' and maybe we should have guessed that Lars Peterson was the target.'

'What had Wally got against Peterson?'

His cousin hesitated for a moment. 'Well, years ago, before we was even born, Wally went a-courtin' of this woman. He was sure sweet on her, accordin' to Pa. But she ups and marries Lars Peterson. Wally just ain't the forgivin' type. He's been gunnin' for Peterson ever since. I reckon that's what it's all about.'

Phil nodded. 'Well, I'll ride out to the ranch tomorrow,' he said. 'If that's all right with the marshal.'

Ed Welsey nodded his consent. He did not feel the need of a deputy to share his moment of glory.

'Sure, you go along, fella,' he said.

'What about us?' Hal Vernon asked meekly. 'We didn't mean to cause trouble, but Wally was family.'

Phil glanced at the marshal. Ed Welsey got up from his chair and went over to the bars. He stood clutching his damaged arm.

'I'll have to speak to the judge,' he said. 'You can't go around threatenin' the law and then walk away. But I'll put in a good word. I don't figure as how it's exactly a hangin' matter.'

Phil had crossed over to the window and was looking out at what was happening on the main street. He turned to face the others with a grim expression on his face.

'It looks as if it could end up that way,' he suggested. 'It might be better if the lads left town tonight. Folk out there are gatherin' and talkin' like politicians at an election. I reckon as how they figure that if Wally was causin' trouble, then young Hal and Vinnie here was helpin' him. Folk don't always think straight and we could have a lynchin' on our hands before the night's out.'

Young Vinnie came over to the bars to join his brother.

'We're Vernons,' he protested. 'They wouldn't do that to us.'

Phil looked at him pityingly. 'Marshal Anderson was popular, and that fella guardin' the stage had a lotta friends in Elverton,' he said in a flat voice.

Ed Welsey glanced out of the window. The street noises were getting louder and folk were gathering around the saloon steps. The marshal swallowed nervously.

'I can't let these fellas go without the mayor's

permission,' he muttered.

Phil shrugged. 'If he hears that noise I don't figure as how you'll be able to find the mayor. He don't want to fall out with folks in town. Or with the ranchers.' He turned to the two prisoners. 'Where are your horses?'

They told him that they were with Wally's chuck wagon. Phil Jones turned to the window again. Marshal Welsey joined him and looked anxiously at the growing signs of trouble.

'I reckon we'd better let them go,' he whispered to Phil. 'You can explain to the mayor. You've got experience with these things.'

'Send them out the rear door,' Phil advised. 'And tell them not to ride back to the Vernon ranch. That would throw suspicion on my Uncle Harry and make things worse. They should travel south and cross the border if necessary.'

Ed Welsey nodded agreement. He went back to the prisoners to explain what was going to happen. They eagerly agreed and slipped out of the back door of the jailhouse a few minutes later. Marshal Welsey looked at Phil and then glanced uncertainly out of the window again.

'I figure as how there ain't nothin' more for us to do now,' he said slowly. 'Things will soon quieten down when the saloon closes. I have to rest my arm and I reckon that you need to get ready to go out to Harry Vernon's place tomorrow.

How about we lock up for the night?'

The deputy nodded silently and the two men soon left the jailhouse and went their separate ways. The town did seem quieter, but there was a reason for it that neither of them knew about.

The two Vernon brothers crept silently along the back lanes to the northern edge of Elverton. As they came out of a narrow alley between two stores, they were confronted by a sight that paralysed their thoughts for a moment.

A ruddy glow lay ahead of them, and when the chuck wagon came into view they could see the flames beginning to leap up from it. A crowd stood around, enjoying the scene. As an oil-lamp suddenly exploded the mob let out a whoop of joy. Wally's mules and the Vernon horses were tethered to a nearby tree, The crowd had taken them and everything else worth stealing from the wagon.

Hal stepped back into the shadow of the buildings.

'Let's get the hell outa here,' he whispered. 'We'll go down the back lanes and try for a coupla horses in one of the corrals.'

'They won't be saddled,' Vinnie objected.

'We ain't in a position to be fussy,' Hal muttered as he pulled his brother back the way they had come.

But they were too late. The glare of the fire got

brighter and somebody in the crowd spotted the moving figures. The mob turned as the two men were recognized. Hal and Vinnie began to run down the dirt-littered alley in total panic. Their guns had been returned to them and both brothers knew that their only way out was to use them. They pulled the weapons from their holsters and turned to take potshots at their pursuers.

The men in the crowd drew their own guns and a hail of bullets split the night air. Hal fell to his knees, recovered for a moment but was hit again. He rolled over while his brother reached a corner and dashed round it out of pistol range. He was alone for a moment, with a view of the lighted main street ahead of him. He had vague thoughts of running back to the jailhouse and demanding the protection of the law. Then he heard footsteps and shouts behind him.

He ran a searching hand along the wooden wall to his left. Any unlocked door could be a source of help. But there was none. Just one shuttered window and a cat that scuttled away as he neared it. He stumbled on some rubbish that bestrewed the alley. As he recovered his balance, several shots rang out. The little lane was lighted by the flashes for a moment. Just long enough for the last of Harry Vernon's sons to see the sudden jet of blood that poured down his chest. He stumbled and hugged the wall as if for comfort. The pursuers closed in and he had a vague vision of faces around him as he collapsed in the filth of the alley.

FOURTEEN

Phil Jones set off as soon as there was enough light in the sky for his horse to find a firm footing on the trail. The wind was sharp and blew grit in his face. Cold penetrated his flapping trail coat, and his eyes watered as he blinked the fine dust away.

It was a long ride to Harry Vernon's place and he needed to occupy the time by thinking of the approach he would have to use. Telling a family member that he had just lost three of his kin was going to be a difficult job. Phil almost wished that the journey would take longer. He stopped for a while to eat and to water his mount. Getting back into the saddle was a reluctant move but he knew it had to be done. The large outline of the ranch house and its surrounding buildings was not a particularly welcome sight. He reined in his horse and sat looking at the place for a moment. Then he gave a deep sigh and spurred forward to meet

Harry Vernon.

His uncle was at the house and came out to greet him with a strange eagerness. He watched the young man dismount and take off the trail coat. Then, after a brief exchange, the rancher led the way into the warm building. There seemed to be nobody else around and Harry Vernon stood in the middle of the well-furnished room and faced his caller.

'Well, I got me a nasty feelin' that you're bringin' bad news, young fella,' he said anxiously. 'Is it about Wally and the lads?'

'You got the right of it, Uncle Harry.'

Phil took the cup of hot coffee that was silently offered and then told his story. The old man listened without moving until it was over. Then he sniffed and his pale eyes seemed to mist over a little.

'So it was Wally,' he said softly as though talking to himself. 'And I sent the lads to town to keep him outa trouble. All gone, and all my work wasted. I feel real guilty about this, Phil. I never thought of Wally havin' the malice to do it. He's ruined every plan I ever had. Killed a dream, he has.'

He sat down heavily in the large leather chair by the empty fireplace.

'And Lars Peterson never figured in it at all,' he mused. 'I should have followed my instinct there.

It just weren't his style. All this killin' started off by an old fool who was still smartin' over somethin' that happened to him more than thirty years ago. I shoulda seen Wally's game, but we was kin, and you don't think badly of your kin, do you?'

'Sometimes you have to think badly of them, Uncle Harry,' Phil said sadly. 'For an instance, I never reckoned on Wally havin' the brains for all this. It needed plannin' and one hell of a lot of money behind it. Buyin' them rifles, for instance. Where would Wally get somethin' like a thousand dollars? And then again, would Marshal Anderson have opened the back door of the jailhouse to Wally? I don't reckon he would. Do you?'

Harry Vernon had been staring into space but the sudden coldness of Phil's words made him narrow his eyes and look hard at his nephew.

'What are you gettin' at, fella?' he snapped.

Phil crossed to the window and looked out across the yard. There was no smoke from the cookhouse and no sign of movement in the outbuildings.

'Where is everybody, Uncle Harry?' he asked.

'The hands is out on the range, and I sent youg Ernie into town to see what the hell was keepin' Hal, Vinnie, and Wally. Why?'

'Well, if you recall what happened to Lars Peterson and his family, you might need all those hands,' Phil said quietly. 'I would figure that word

152

has got out to Vic Lawrence and the other ranchers about the rustlin' and the killin' of Marshal
Anderson. They're gonna be payin' you a call in
the next few days.'

Harry jumped out of his chair. 'It ain't my fault,'
he whined in an almost panicky voice. 'I never
wanted them to raid the Peterson spread. I tried to
hold them back. You know that.'

'Wally needed help to do what he did, Uncle
Harry. The only hands he could use for the
rustlin' were the folk he worked with right here.
Your hands. And it were not Wally as killed the
marshal.'

'Then who the hell was it?' the rancher bawled.

'You, Uncle Harry.'

There was a long silence. The rancher stood by
the table staring into space. Phil Jones stayed at
the window, looking out at the birds feeding on
fallen grain. He turned to glance at his uncle and
the old man suddenly burst into laughter. He
came across to slap his nephew on the arm in a
friendly fashion.

'So I couldn't fool you, young fella,' he crowed.
'Well, I always did say you was the brains of the
family. You're right, boy. I organized everythin'
from beginnin' to end. It ain't ended as I wished,
but I sure as hell tried. You could have been in
with me, and between us, we woulda got away with
it. But now it's all gone wrong.'

153

He had slowly moved over to a large mahogany dresser and now opened one of the drawers. He drew a Colt .44 and pointed it at Phil.

'You ain't gonna talk, young fella,' he said grimly. 'I can settle things with other folk as long as they don't get the whole story from you. Oh, I figure that you've worked everythin' out. But nobody saw you arrive here, and folk might just think you left town to go back to Phoenix and run your hotel.'

Phil grinned. 'I left a letter back in town,' he said. 'It tells the entire story. And them other ranchers ain't gonna be in anythin' but a killin' mood when they get the real tale. So just put that gun away.'

'And go back to the jailhouse with you? I don't aim to be tried and hanged in some clapboard town like Elverton.'

'I ain't takin' you back to the jailhouse, Uncle Harry. I came here to give you the chance you never gave Lars Peterson. Just ride out while you still can.'

The gun wavered. Harry Vernon looked at his nephew and then his glance seemed to stray to the green bulk of the small safe that stood next to the Chicago organ.

'Are you playin' me straight?' he asked sharply.
'Yes.'
'And that letter?'

154

'The judge only opens it if I don't get back safely to Elverton. Your life and my life are kinda joined together right now.'

The old rancher chuckled as if he suddenly appreciated the stand-off.

'So it would seem,' he acknowledged. 'So tell me what you know.'

Phil crossed to the nearest chair and sat down. The rancher sat opposite him and the revolver rested on his bony knee.

'I knew that Marshal Anderson would only open the door to somebody he really knew and trusted. Somebody who was a friend. You were the one who killed him and took his prisoner. You had Wally pose as Lars Peterson and the man naturally believed him. But what you wanted from the fella was the name of the man who had told about the money on the stage. That's why you was comin' outa the bank with such a smile on your face. You'd made a deal with Will Halliday for as big a loan as you needed to buy more land.'

The rancher nodded.

'You're right, son,' he agreed. 'I had that money-lender across a saddle. He couldn't offer me a deal fast enough. And then I ordered them guns addressed to Peterson, and we went on with the rustlin' week after week. Always keepin' clear of Peterson's spread so that folk would eventually ask why his cattle were never stole. And they did ask, and Wally was eager to tell them. It was as good a plan as you could wish for. The other ranchers were doin' the work for me. And with Les Weldon wantin' to sell up, I was gonna get more land than anyone round here had ever owned.'

'Yep, and you wanted me to help you do it.'

'Them two boys of mine was just gunslingers. I needed you, fella. I wanted to be somebody. Establish somethin' in the territory. Leave a name behind me, and show that a Vernon had really made it big. Is that too much of a dream?'

'Killin' folks is a nightmare, Uncle Harry. They hang you for it. How did you switch horses at Reg Strode's place?'

The rancher grinned. 'Wally or one of the hands picked up a cow pony with the Peterson brand. After you shoved that hold-up fella into the jailhouse, they just changed his horse for the one we wanted one of Peterson's hands to find. And Wally mentioned it to him in the saloon. Said he'd seen a Peterson brand in Reg Strode's corrals. It was all like them stage conjurers. Wally did the same sorta trick when Reg shot that fella. He fussed over him and slipped that prayer book into his pocket. It was so easy. And we'd torn pages outa the book and left them at that creek for some smart young deputy to find.'

'And I was the rube who fell for it,' Phil said

with a reluctant grin.

Harry nodded. 'That's right, lad. You see, clever folks like you don't always think that other fellas might not be so simple. So what happens now?'

'I reckon as how that safe there is stuffed with plenty of ready cash, Uncle Harry,' Phil said. 'A wise man would scoop it all up, load a rig with what he needed, and get the hell out. Them other ranchers could be on their way pretty soon. And when your own hands hear about Wally and the two lads, they're gonna light out before the law comes lookin' for them.'

Harry sighed heavily. 'You could be right, lad,' he said sadly. 'Will you help me pack? There's a four-wheeled rig over in the stable and I use them two palominos that are in the near paddock. Get 'em ready for me, will you?'

Phil left the house and Harry Vernon opened the safe with a trembling hand.

Phil Jones got back to town two days later. He tethered his pony to the rail at the jailhouse and mounted the stoop to report to the marshal. The door was locked and the place shuttered up. He hesitated for a moment and then went down the street to the mayor's store. It was also shuttered and locked up. The young deputy stood bewildered by events. He looked up and down the main street at the faces of the few people who were around in the heat of the afternoon. They gave him polite nods but seemed wary.

Phil decided to go round to the judge's house. He would not yet have made his daily pilgrimage to the saloon and would be approachable. The white gate was already open and he went up the path and knocked at the glass-panelled door. Mrs Murphy opened it and greeted him warmly. She was a little woman, skinny and pale, but with a bright smile and starched skirts that rustled.

She led him into the main room where the judge sat in an armchair with a cup of coffee in his hand.

'Well, young fella,' he greeted the new arrival, 'I was wonderin' about you. Almost lookin' forward to openin' that letter and gettin' all the dirt on the local villains. Give the lad a cuppa coffee, Ma. He looks as if he's done some hard travellin' this day.'

He leaned forward in his chair.

'You broke the news to poor Harry?' he asked.

'Yes, and he was real upset by it,' Phil said in a neutral voice.

'I can imagine. A sad thing to lose two sons and a fella who might be your brother if stories is true.'

'What's been happenin' in town?' Phil asked as Ma Murphy came in with his coffee.

'Well, we've lost a mayor and a marshal.' The judge chuckled. 'When folks found out that the Vernon boys was let outa jail, they got pretty riled.

There was a council meetin' and the mayor was thrown outa office. His marshal went with him. I guess they had to leave town. Folk wouldn't go into the store, and Ma Raynor felt mighty shamed at not bein' queen of the sewin' circle no more.'

He leaned across to Phil and gave a wide grin.

'We're havin' an election for a mayor next week,' he said warmly, 'and we'll sure as hell be needin' a new marshal. You're just the fella for the job, young man.'

Phil Jones stood up to go.

'Sorry I can't help you there, Judge,' he said regretfully, 'but I'm inclined to think that I'll be too busy runnin' the biggest spread in the territory.